THE

BOX

HOUSE

By

Susan L. Paré

THE BOX HOUSE by Susan L. Paré

Printed in the United States of America.
First Edition: 2020.7
All rights reserved.
Cover designed by Susan L. Paré
ISBN-13: 978-1-7335572-6-9

MORE BY THIS AUTHOR

The Proof Is In the Pudding

Blueberries and Bears and My Brother's Shoes

Red, White, and Blue (A Short Story)

She Never Stopped Talking

Red

The House on Ludington Street

What's Behind the Screen Door?

The Mayor's Son

Willerton Woods

Cowtown

Floating Face Down
A Sheriff "Cowboy" Berkson Mystery Novel – Book Three

Let's Play Autopsy

A Bad Week In Hollister
A Sheriff "Cowboy" Berkson Mystery Novel – Book Two

Don't Smother Your Mother
A Sheriff "Cowboy" Berkson Mystery Novel – Book One

Crossing Sydney

THE BOX HOUSE by Susan L. Paré

Index

Acknowledgment

I would like to thank Aaron Holbrook, Regional Editor of CJ News, for permission to use this picture. This article appeared in the Columbus Journal sometime in the early 1950s.

A STRUCTURE WHICH has startled the eyes of many motorists passing through the Columbus area is the house on the rabbit ranch, about three miles east of Columbus. The tall, slender house was originally a look-out, built high on the ridge, overlooking what originally was a fox farm.

THE BOX HOUSE by Susan L. Paré

THE
BOX
HOUSE

THE BOX HOUSE by Susan L. Paré

Chapter One

"So, what do you think?" Mark Starckweather asked his client. He couldn't read her - couldn't tell what she was thinking. He usually knew immediately if a buyer was interested in a property he was showing – especially this property - or if they just wanted to get the hell back in their car and drive away. But not this one. Not only did her face express absolutely no emotion but her body language was impossible to read.

Samantha continued to stare at the house, not answering him. "Except for the shape of the house, I don't see anything remarkable about it," she finally commented. "Is the inside of the house as bad as the outside?"

"Would you like to go in and see for yourself?"

"In a minute. I'd like to take a look at the back of the house first, if you don't mind."

"No problem, Mrs. Carlson."

"Please, call me Samantha. And, you can drop the missus. I'm not married."

"Of course. Samantha it is." He pointed to a two-car garage. "The garage is the newest structure on the property. I believe it was built around 1960. The two smaller buildings over there were originally used as a tool shed and a chicken coop," he told her, indicating two buildings located to the back and right of the house.

"Is it hard to raise chickens?" Samantha asked.

"I'm not sure. To tell you the truth, I've never thought about it. I figure most people who lived back then kept a few chickens if they wanted eggs. You couldn't just run to the grocery store like you do today."

"Of course," she replied, already losing interest in chickens. "When did you say this house was built? I seem to recall it was the early 1900s."

"You're right. It was built in 1910."

"What about that one?" Samantha asked as she pointed to a small barn set farther back on the property.

"That one was built the same year as the house. It was probably home for some pigs and a few horses. They may have had a few cows, too. For their milk, you know."

"That must be what that stink is," Samantha declared.

"I don't smell anything," Starckweather said, looking confused by her comment.

"Well, maybe you should get your nose checked. I smell something that smells like shit."

"Mrs. Carl..." He hesitated. "Sorry, I mean Samantha. Seriously, I don't smell anything. It's been years since anyone kept any farm animals here."

"Well, I smell something. Never mind. It's not important." She turned and looked at the house. "I guess we should go check out the inside of the house. However, I would like to see what the inside of these old buildings looks like before we leave. You know, to see if they are worth keeping or if they will have to be torn down."

"Of course," Starckweather replied. "I'm anxious to see what you think of the inside. It's quite different from anything I've listed before."

"Well, let's go take a look," she said.

An hour later Mark Starckweather and Samantha

Carlson walked out the front door. Mark locked the door, then turned the handle and pushed to be sure the lock was secure. He turned to Samantha and smiled. "Well, what do you think?"

Samantha took a deep breath of fresh air. "It smells pretty musty in there."

"Well, it has been closed up for a while. I guess I should remember to air it out before I have a showing."

Samantha grinned. "It wouldn't hurt."

"Well?" he asked again."

"In a million years, I never would have guessed that the inside of this house would look like that."

"The people who bought it in 1960 put a fortune into it."

"It's a beautiful home inside. Of course, it needs some work. All the rooms could use fresh paint and some of the wood needs refinishing. But that's mostly cosmetic stuff. What I don't understand is why the outside is so..." She shrugged her shoulders. "I guess the only word I can use is ugly."

"Do you still want to look at the outbuildings before we leave?" Mark asked her, hoping to change the subject.

"Why didn't anyone do anything about the outside? It doesn't look like it's had a new coat of paint since forever. I'm really curious as to why it's been neglected so badly."

"It has been a while since it's been painted. I guess most of the people who lived here didn't stay long enough to fix up the outside or they didn't have the money. Plus, there were a lot of renters who lived here."

"But, certainly those people who spent so much money on the inside would have done something about it. I don't understand unless..." She smiled. "Are you keeping something from me?"

Starckweather looked away. "It's a long story. Their plans for the house fell apart and they stopped the remodeling. They had pretty much finished the inside at that point and were about to start on the outside. Anyway, they walked away. It stayed empty for a while after that."

"I see. Exactly how many people have lived here?"

"It's an old house. It's seen a lot of families come and go throughout the years."

"Well, someone had to have painted it since 1910."

"Of course, it's been painted since then. But, it's probably been around twenty years since the last time."

"So, tell me a little more about the house."

"What do you want to know?"

"Everything that you know."

"That's a lot. Do you actually have an interest in purchasing this property? Because I have other homes I can show you."

"I might be." She smiled. "Actually, I am. But, before I commit to anything, I want more information. You know, full disclosure and all. I'm a curious person and I want to know more about this house's history."

"It's an old house, Samantha. There's a lot of history."

"I have the time. Perhaps we could go back to your office and you could give me the lowdown."

"I can do that. Just let me lock up."

"You did already," Samantha reminded him.

"Right," Mark said grinning. "I guess I'm getting old and forgetful." Mark pulled his car keys out of his

4

pocket and unlocked his car. He opened the door for Samantha and helped her into the passenger side of the car. "How long are you going to be in town?" he asked as he shut the car door.

Samantha watched him walk to the driver's side of the car and get in. "Why?" she inquired.

"Because it's a long story."

He put the car in reverse and backed out of the driveway.

"Wait a minute," Samantha said. "I want to get a picture."

"There's a picture on the flyer I gave you," Mark said.

"This house looks nothing like the picture on the flyer, Mark. That picture's been touched up. You know that."

Mark put the car in park and waited as Samantha opened the door and jumped out of the car.

"It looks like a big oblong box standing on end, doesn't it," she called out, as she snapped a few pictures on her cell phone.

"I guess," Mark replied. "It's been called the Box House forever."

"Well, the name fits, doesn't it?" she said as she got back into the car.

"It's called that for more than one reason," Mark told her, grinning.

"Oh, really?" Why is that?"

"The person who built the house back in 1910 was named Box. John Box."

"Are you serious? Is that why he built it like that? Because of his name?"

"No. He built it like that so he could stand watch

over his property."

Samantha glanced over at him. "For what reason did he..."

"Are you hungry?" Mark asked, interrupting her.

"I guess I could eat something."

"Great. Let's pick up some carry-out before we go back to my office."

"Sounds good to me," Samantha said agreeing with him.

"Is Culver's okay with you?"

"That's fine."

"By the way, you never told me how long you plan to be in town."

"I guess it all depends on how long it takes you to tell me the story about this house," she replied, smiling.

"Would you like some more Coke?" Mark asked as he refilled his glass.

"I'm good, thanks." Samantha wiped her mouth with her napkin, sat back, and smiled. "All right. Out with it. Tell me everything."

Mark looked at his watch and frowned.

"Is there someplace you need to be?" Samantha asked.

"I didn't realize it was so late. I can give you the short version now if you want."

"I prefer the long version."

"I have an appointment for another showing in half an hour. Perhaps, we could do this later?"

"I'll be in town for the next few days, Mark. Of course, we can do this later. Go do your thing."

"Are you sure?"

"Positive. What do you have going on tomorrow?"

"My day is pretty much open. I could meet you here around nine?"

"That sounds good." Samantha stood up. "Give me a call if anything changes. I'm staying at the Century II Motel."

"How is that place?"

"It's okay. It's clean enough, but it needs to be updated. Is that the only motel in town?"

"This is a small town. I don't think there's a need for more than one motel."

"I disagree. Anyway, I'll see you tomorrow. I think I'll drive around for a while and take in the sights."

"That should take about five minutes."

Samantha drove back to the house, pulled her car over to the side of the road, put it in park, and turned off the ignition. She pushed her long dark hair back out of her eyes and stared at the property.

After a few moments, she got out of her car, ran across the road, and up a small embankment. She stopped and looked at the tall weird-looking house, wondering if she was crazy for pursuing this. "Well, crazy or not, it's gonna happen," she mumbled to herself.

Chapter Two

(1910)

John Box pulled a dirty hanky out of his overalls pocket and wiped the sweat from his forehead. "Pretty damn hot for September," he called out to his brother, Peter, who was picking some nails up off the ground.

"I guess," Peter replied. "Are we about done?"

"We're never done, Peter. You know that. The work never ends."

"I mean, are we done for today? I'd like to clean up."

"Are you going over to that woman's house again?"

"She asked me for supper. I don't want to be late."

John grinned. "Then, by all means, be off with ya. You don't want to keep her waiting."

"Thanks, John." Peter put the nails he was holding into a paper bag and pulled off his gloves. "I'll just go wash up, then," he said and walked away.

John Box studied the outside of the house, looking to see if any spot was lacking paint. Peter was a good enough worker but he had a tendency to daydream and often slacked off on the job. John grinned, thinking that was usually true after he had spent the night with that widow

"Not bad," he muttered. He had been living here with his family for almost six months. It had taken his brother the last two months to paint the house but he had done a good job. John was proud of him. Just a little more work on the building

that housed the rabbit cages, and it would be ready for paint. John hoped it would be completed before the weather turned cold.

"Daddy, daddy," a child's voice called out. "Can I pet them?"

"No, Gretchen, you may not," John answered her sternly. "These rabbits are not to be played with. You go play with your dolly."

"But, I want to play with the bunnies," Gretchen whined. "You play with them. Why can't I?"

"I don't play with them, child. I feed them and clean out their cages, but I don't play with them."

"I saw you pet one," she declared, pouting.

"It never happened. You're imagining things. Now run along. I have work to do."

"Please," she begged him. "Just one."

John looked down at his little daughter and sighed. "Go find your mother."

Gretchen stuck out her lower lip and looked down at the ground. "She's busy."

"Well, so am I. Now, scat."

"Just one little pet? Pleeaase."

John reached down and picked her up. "One pet. Understand?" He walked over to the cages, opened one, reached in, and pulled out a large brown rabbit.

Rachel giggled and laid her little hand on the rabbit's back. She gently stroked it, smiling. "He's soft, Daddy."

"All right. That's enough," John said after a few moments

and put the rabbit back into its cage. He set his daughter down and started to walk away.

"Daddy?"

Sighing, he turned and looked at Gretchen. "What now, girl?"

"Thank you, daddy."

John Box had no sons. Gretchen was his only child and try as he might not to spoil her, he knew she could wrap him around her little finger.

His brother, Peter, lived with him and his family but John figured it was only a matter of time before Peter would marry and move out. However, if he was lucky, his brother would continue to work with him and share in the profits of the rabbit farm.

Raising rabbits wasn't a hard job but a person needed to be vigilant in watching over them. On many occasions, some predators such as a fox or a raccoon managed to get a hutch door open and escape with a rabbit in its jaws. John hoped that once the building that housed the rabbits was completed, no predator would be able to get at the rabbits.

"Supper is ready."

John turned and smiled at the woman standing behind him. "I didn't hear you come up on me," he told her.

Martha grinned. "Well, you know what they say, don't you? The hearing is the first thing to go."

"What's on the menu tonight?"

"Chicken. I killed that old hen that stopped laying. Although, I need to warn you that the meat may be a little

tough."

"I imagine it will be. Old hens are almost always tough. Look at you," he said grinning.

Martha punched him playfully on his arm and laughed. "Be careful what you say, old man."

"Old? I'm still a youngster. How can you call me old?"

Martha sighed. "You're almost forty."

"Well, so are you."

"That may be; however, I'm growing better with age, my darling."

John laughed. "I can't argue with that." He put his arm around her as they walked towards the house. "Has Peter left yet?"

"He did. Didn't you see him?"

"I must have had my back turned."

"It looks like the eyes are the second thing to go," Martha replied teasingly.

"I'm on alert tonight," John said.

"I know. I'll take the first few hours so you can get some rest."

"We can't afford to lose more rabbits and chickens."

"It will be better when we get the watchdog," Martha commented.

"Let's hope so."

"At least the chickens scream their heads off and try to warn us when a fox is near."

"So do the rabbits. We just don't hear them," John said.

Chapter Three

_(1923)_

"You're what?" John Box yelled. "For God's sake, Gretchen, you're just a child yourself."

Gretchen hung her head in shame, not capable of looking at her father. "I'm so sorry, Father."

Martha glanced at her daughter, feeling a little sick to her stomach. She had feared something like this might happen. Now she blamed herself for not saying something to John earlier.

John glared at the young man sitting next to Gretchen on the couch. "You! You have disgraced my daughter! I should shoot you and feed you to the pigs. No one would blame me after what you've done."

Ray Slitzer looked at John Box and shrugged. "I'm sorry, Mr. Box, but I didn't force her, you know. She wanted to do it."

Gretchen's head jerked up, her face showing shock at his statement. "No. You made me."

"Is that true? Did you rape my daughter?"

"No. I never..." He turned to Gretchen. "How could you say that? You know that ain't true."

John walked to the end of the living room, turned, and walked back to where Ray was sitting. "I took you in and gave you a job when nobody else would. I trusted you and this is the thanks I get," he cried out, trying to control his temper.

"I said I was sorry. Hey, I'll marry her if that's what you

want."

John raised his hand, intent on slapping the young man.

"John, don't," Martha cried out.

John hesitated and stepped back. "I should kill you for what you've done."

"You two will get married, of course," Martha said. "You can live here and Ray will continue to work on the farm. We have plenty of room for a little person." She sighed. "What has happened is shameful. But, like my mother used to say, no sense in crying over spilled milk. Nothing will change except that you'll be married." She looked at her husband. "John, can you live with that?"

John stared at Ray. "I don't have much of a choice, do I?" He turned away and wiped his eyes. "We'll see how it goes."

"Thank you, John," Martha said.

"I'm going for a walk," John declared. As he started to leave the room, he turned and looked at his daughter. "You..." His voice broke with emotion. "You... You have broken my heart."

Gretchen stared at him for a moment. "I'm so so sorry, Father," she said, as tears filled her eyes and she started to cry. "If I could take it back, I would. You know I would never want to hurt you."

"Too late," John said softly as he walked out of the room.

Ray grinned and put his arm around Gretchen. "Looks like we're gonna get hitched, baby girl."

Sobbing now, Gretchen pulled away from him and stood up. "I hate you and I hate what you did to me," she cried out as she ran out of the room.

"What's wrong with her?" Ray asked Martha. "I said I'd marry her."

"How can you be so stupid? You're walking a fine line here and you better watch your step," Martha said. "John is a good man and a patient man. But, he also has a breaking point and he's close to it right now. So, don't push him. Ray, because I can guarantee you will regret it."

"I seen him get angry before," Ray told her. "It wasn't no worse than when my old man gets mad. Now, he really has a temper. I ain't afraid of John."

Martha got up out of her chair and walked over to Ray. She gazed down at him. "Look at me," she demanded.

Ray slowly raised his head and looked into her eyes. "What?"

"It would be wise to be afraid of him. You have no idea what that man is capable of," she told him, speaking softly. "No matter what your father did to you, it is only a small percentage of what John is capable of."

"I didn't mean..."

"Hush," Martha whispered. "I'm talking. Now, I want you to remember what I just told you."

"I got it," Ray mumbled. "John is a badass."

The sound of the slap echoed through the room. Startled, Ray put his hand to his face and yelled out. "Whatcha do that for?"

"You need to learn to respect your elders, Ray. You have a smart mouth and that will be dealt with. Now, what do you have to say?"

Ray looked confused. "About what?"

"What do you say to a person when you've stepped out of line?"

Ray shrugged. "I don't know. Sorry?"

"Now you're getting the idea," Martha told him, as she stared at him.

"I'm sorry, ma'am?"

"Is that a question?"

"No ma'am. I'm sorry I didn't respect you."

Martha smiled. "Now, that wasn't so hard, was it?"

"I guess not."

Ray stood up and looked at her. "I still ain't afraid of John."

"Sit – back - down," Martha demanded. "We aren't done here."

"What now?" Ray whined as he plopped back onto the couch.

"I want you to imagine the worst thing that John could do to you if he got really angry." She waited for a moment. "Are you imagining it?"

"I guess."

"Good. Now think of it being ten times more horrible. Are you picturing it?"

"I guess," Ray said again, smirking as he turned his head away.

"You guess?"

"Well, it's hard, you know. Imagining stuff and all," he told her, grinning.

"Is something funny?"

"No, ma'am," he replied, stifling a laugh.

"Forget about John. Close your eyes." She waited. "I said close your eyes."

"All right, I'm closing them."

"Imagine you're naked and you're in hell," she said, her voice so soft it was barely a whisper. "Fire is cascading down from above and onto your body. Your skin is slowly being peeled off strip by strip, while dogs gnaw at your penis..."

"Mrs. Box, I'm not..."

"Quiet!" she ordered. She looked at Ray who was staring at her. "I'm beginning to lose patience with you. Close your eyes." She waited until Ray closed his eyes

"Your skin is slowly being peeled off strip by strip while dogs gnaw at your penis," she repeated. "You're on your hands and knees being raped over and over by dozens of the devil's angels. Fire ants are crawling into your ears and although you try to scream..."

"Stop!" Ray cried out. "That's enough. I get the picture."

"Do you, Ray? Because, if you think that John is a badass, there's nothing that he could do compared to what I will do to you if you ever hurt my daughter. Now get out of here. You have chores to do."

Ray jumped off the couch and ran out of the room, running into Gretchen.

"What's the matter with you? You look like you've seen a ghost?"

Ray stared at her. "Your mother is fucking nuts."

Chapter Four

(1925)

"Please don't tell father."

Martha looked at her daughter, tears swelling in her eyes. "I'll kill him for doing this to you."

"It was my fault. I started complaining..."

"About his drinking. Right?" Gretchen interrupted. "You need to leave him, Gretchen, before he kills you."

"He's under so much pressure, Mother. He can't find a job anywhere."

"Well, your father won't hire him again. He gave him more than enough chances."

"I know. He promised me he won't hit me again."

Martha shook her head. "But, he will. You know that and so do I."

"I have some news." Gretchen looked away and stared out the bedroom window.

Martha took a sip of her tea and put the cup down. "Please don't tell me you're pregnant again."

"I am. It's about time that Luke has a little sister or brother. I don't want him to be an only child."

"How can you even let that man touch you?" Martha asked, shaking her head in disgust.

"Do you think I have a choice?" Gretchen asked her mother, looking away. "Besides, he's not always mean. It's only when he has too much to drink."

17

"I should never have allowed you to move out of this house. At least when you lived here I could protect you."

"And, I appreciate that, Mother, but Ray and I need to have our own place. Besides, we're just across the street."

"And, that's still too far away. I'm going to ask your father to talk to him. You're pregnant and he's beating on you. This has to stop."

"Please, don't say anything. It won't happen again. I promise. Just be happy for me that I'm going to have another baby."

Martha patted Gretchen's hand. "You poor thing. I don't know what I would have done if your father had ever hit me. It's just not right. I'm going to talk to Ray."

"No, he'll just get mad and take it out on me."

"You know you and Luke can always come back here and live with us."

"Did they?" Samantha asked Mark Starckweather.

"Are you sure you don't want more than coffee?" Mark asked her, ignoring her question. "I can guarantee you that you've never had eggs like they make here."

"Just coffee is fine. Although, I could go for a bagel with some cream cheese."

Mark held up his hand and motioned for Suzie to come over to the table.

"Whattaya need?" Suzie asked as she approached their table. "More coffee?"

"Do you have any bagels?" Samantha asked.

"Sure do, hon. Do you want one?"

"Please, with cream cheese."

18

"We have regular, strawberry, and pineapple cream cheese. Which one?"

"Pineapple sounds good."

"Sure thing. I'll be right back."

"You were saying that Martha told Gretchen she could come live with her and John. What happened?"

"She stayed with Ray, living in a little run-down house that they rented across the street from her folks."

"I don't understand how she could stay with him," Samantha said. "I'd never stay with a man who hit me."

"Remember that it was a long time ago. Women didn't leave their husbands and get divorced back then. They stuck with it through the good and the bad."

"I guess. Go on with the story."

"Well, despite the beatings, Gretchen stayed with Ray. She named her second son Ezekiel. I heard that by the early 1940s, John had given up on rabbits and had started raising mink. He did quite well financially."

"What about Peter? Did he marry that widow?"

"Ah, yes. Poor Peter. He kinda gets lost in the story. No, he never married the widow woman he had courted."

"Courted?" Samantha said grinning.

"Yes, courted. That's what they did back then. They courted," he stated emphatically. "Anyway, he continued to live with John and Martha until he died."

"When was that?"

"I think it was around 1930 or so. I'm not sure. He was young though. Perhaps 45 or 50. He died a horrible death."

"How so?"

"He was pitching hay from the loft in the barn when he tripped. He fell from the loft and landed on a pitchfork that was sticking out of a bale of hay and was impaled. It took him until the next morning to die. From what I understand, it was pretty gruesome."

"That must have hurt," Samantha muttered softly.

Mark glanced over at her wondering if she was being flippant but decided by the look on her face that she was serious. "I guess. Are you ready to go back out to the house and take another look?"

"I am so ready," she replied. "Let's go."

Mark put on his right turn signal, turned right, and headed down River Road towards the house.

"I drove out here after I left your office yesterday," Samantha told him.

"I figured you would."

"I just walked around for a while. I wanted to see if it would speak to me. You know, sometimes places seem to have a way of letting you know if you belong or not."

"How did that work out for you?" Mark asked, smiling.

"That pig shit smell is still there."

As fast as it had appeared, the grin left Mark's face. "There is no way. There haven't been pigs on that property for sixty years. Plus, there are no farms close by that have pigs on them."

"If you say so."

"When the mink farm was there it smelled horrible. They're stinky little animals. But, Samantha, I just can't figure out what you smell. I don't know what to say." He was quiet for a few moments. "Besides, how do you know what you smell is even pig shit? Have you had a lot of experience smelling pig shit in your lifetime?" he asked her, grinning.

"Maybe."

He glanced over at her. "No, you haven't. Maybe, what you smell is just good old-fashioned country air. Here we are," Mark declared, as he turned left and pulled onto the property.

"Do you have any other appointments this morning?"

"Nope. My calendar is clear. I'm all yours. In fact, if you're interested, I've got a couple more houses I can show you if you decide to pass on this one."

"I don't think so, Mark. It's gonna be this one or none. Smell and all."

Chapter Five

(1941)

    Gretchen lay on the floor whimpering as she waited for the beating to end. Her hands covered her face, protecting it from his filthy pig shit-covered boots. He never aimed for her face. However, on more than one occasion, when he was falling down couldn't see straight drunk and his aim was bad, her face got the brunt of his anger. Regardless, good aim or bad aim, he always finished with what was supposed to be a kick to the ribs.

    "What the hell do ya think you're doing?" Ray suddenly yelled.

    "Step away from my daughter!"

    Gretchen pulled her hands away from her face and glanced up. Her mother was standing in the doorway pointing a 12 gauge shotgun at Ray. She pushed herself up into a sitting position and shook her head no. "Don't do it," she mumbled.

    Ray took a step towards Martha and reached for the gun. "Gimme that gun, you bitch. Who the hell do ya think ya are pointing a gun at me?"

    Martha backed away from him and raised the shotgun a little higher. "Step back, Ray. I'm not afraid of you," she yelled. "Haven't you had enough of his crap, Gretchen?" she asked her daughter, never taking her eyes off of Ray. "This is going to end now!"

    Gretchen looked at her mother, tears streaming down her cheeks. "Don't...."

"Just say the word, Gretchen. Do you want me to pull the trigger, 'cause I will? Yes or no?"

"I can't . . ."

Suddenly Ray staggered backward, hitting the wall behind him with his shoulder. He caught himself as his right leg buckled and he started to fall. He stared at the wall for a moment. "Who the hell put that there?" he mumbled drunkenly. He straightened up and shook his head as if trying to clear out the cobwebs. He turned and looked at his mother-in-law. "You better put that damn gun down."

"Or what? Are you gonna beat me, too? Now hear this, you piece of shit. This is the last time you will ever hit my daughter. I want you out of this house. Now!"

"Well, listen to you. You think you're so tough 'cause you're holding a gun? You're just..."

"Shut up! Just shut the fuck up!" Martha screamed at him.

Gretchen's mouth dropped open, shocked at her mother's language.

Ray laughed. "I didn't know you had it in you. It looks like you're no holier than thou after all," Ray said, sarcastically. "Did you hear that, Gretchen? Your old lady has got quite the mouth on her, don't she?"

Martha looked at Gretchen, tears filling her eyes. "For god's sake, Gretchen, look at this pig. How can you stand being in the same room with him? He smells worse than a stinkin' pigsty."

"Thass it," Ray bellowed as he stumbled towards Martha.

The sound of the shot reverberated throughout the room

followed by Gretchen's terrifying scream as Ray's blood splattered her bruised aching body.

"What have you done?" Gretchen cried out.

"What I should have done a long time ago. He's not gonna hurt you again."

Gretchen reached for her mother's hand. "Help me up." She stood and looked at her husband's body. "He looks dead. Do you think he's dead?"

"Well, seeing as how there's a hole in his chest big enough to put your fist through, I'd say that's a good possibility."

Gretchen stared at the body. "He is one ugly son of a bitch, isn't he?"

"You mean was. He's dead."

"She stared at Ray's body for a few more seconds and suddenly shuddered. "Yes, indeed. He really is one dead ugly son of a bitch." She stepped away from him and sat down on her bed. "Mom?"

"Yes, baby?"

"I'm scared," she said as the tears started to flow.

"Hush, baby. Mama's here. Everything's going to be okay." She wrapped her arms around her daughter and hugged her.

Gretchen pulled back and stared into her mother's eyes. "What are we gonna do now?" she asked.

"Go get your father."

"Like this?" she asked. "I can't go out like this? I'm covered with blood."

"Your right. You go clean up. I'll be right back."

24

John looked up as Martha ran towards him. "What's wrong?" he cried out. "You look like you've seen a ghost."

"I've done something horrible, John. You need to come with me."

"What is it? Did something happen to Gretchen?"

Martha grabbed John's hand and pulled. "Hurry," she hollered. "Run!"

He followed her across the road to Gretchen's house. As they entered the house, Martha turned to John and looked into his eyes. "Please don't hate me. I had no choice."

"What is it, woman?"

"Upstairs. He's up there. Come with me."

"Did Martha go to prison for killing Ray?" Samantha asked as they walked out of the café.

"Nope. No one else found out about it until she died. The police never did put much effort into finding him. Everyone just kind of figured he took off."

"How do you know all this?"

"Martha confessed to killing Ray on her deathbed. Years later, a journal was found that Gretchen had kept. It pretty much highlighted what I've told you. I believe most of it is true."

"What happened to Gretchen?"

"After Ray was killed, Gretchen moved back in with her parents. She lived with them until they passed away.

Neither one spoke for a moment.

"It rained last night," Samantha said.

"I know. The thunder woke me. It's gonna be

muddy out there. I'm glad to see you're wearing sensible shoes."

"You can't go wrong with a good pair of sneakers."

Mark turned left, up a small incline, and stopped his car alongside the house. "Are you ready for the tour?"

Samantha smiled. "I'm so ready. But, before..."

"Yes?"

"What happened to Ray's body?"

(1941)

"I don't know what else to tell you," Gretchen told the police officer. *"He just left and hasn't come back."*

"And, that was three days ago?" Officer Roberts asked.

"Yes, Sir."

"Why did you wait so long to contact us?"

"Officer, you know Ray," Martha said. "You know how he is when he drinks. We thought he was on another bender and sleeping it off somewhere. This isn't the first time that Ray hasn't come home after being out all night."

"But, you waited three days. That would have to be a pretty heavy bender."

"I think he is seeing another woman," Gretchen told him, looking away. "I thought he was with her."

Officer Roberts looked surprised. "I haven't heard any gossip about Ray carrying on with anyone. Is she from around here? Who is it?"

Gretchen shrugged. "I have no idea. But, there have been a few times when he's come home smelling of perfume, and one time he had lipstick smeared on his collar."

26

"What about Luke and Zeke? Do they have any idea where their dad could be?"

"Luke's in Germany," Gretchen told him.

"That's right. I forgot that he enlisted. What about Zeke? Does he know anything?"

"I doubt it. He and his grandpa are up north hunting. They won't be back until tomorrow."

Officer Roberts wrote something in his notebook and closed it. "Well, that's about it. If you hear from him, let me know. In the meantime, I'll put the word out to the neighboring towns to keep an eye open."

"Thank you, Officer Roberts," Gretchen said.

"Ma'am." He tipped his hat and walked out the door.

"What do you think, Mother? Could you tell I was nervous? Could you see me shaking?"

"Relax. You did fine, Gretchen. I have an idea that Officer Roberts will make a few calls and that will be that."

"I think I should wait a while before Zeke and I move back in with you and father. What do you think?

"You should probably keep the house for another month or so before you give your landlord notice."

"There's something else, Mother."

Martha looked at her and sighed. "Again?"

"I'm afraid so."

"I'll get the crib out of the attic and clean it up. How far along are you?"

"A few months. She's due at the end of April."

"She?" Martha asked, looking puzzled. "Exactly how do you know it's a girl?"

"I just know."

"It would be nice to have a little girl around," Martha said. She looked around the house and frowned. "Why don't you stay with me again tonight? I don't like it when you're all alone in this house."

"Thank you, Mother. I think I will."

"Your father and Zeke will be home tomorrow. You'll need to keep it together so Zeke doesn't suspect anything."

"I know and I will. Do you think this will be hard on the boys?"

"What's that?"

"Not having a dad anymore."

"I doubt they'll notice he's gone."

"Mother! How can you say that?"

"He was a horrible father and you know it, Gretchen. His death is not a great loss to anyone."

"I guess. Still, it's hard to wrap my head around the fact that he's dead and won't hurt us again. It hasn't sunk in yet that I don't have to be afraid all the time."

"It's a good thing."

Gretchen smiled. "I've got a few chores to do. I'll come over after that."

Martha kissed her daughter on the cheek and walked to the door. "Supper's at the usual time," she called out.

"I'll be there," Gretchen replied.

Chapter Six

"What happened to the building where the rabbits were housed?"

"It burned down a long time ago. I remember my dad telling me about it. It was a fox farm at the time of the fire."

Samantha looked at the ground as she walked, trying to avoid as many small puddles as possible. "Tell me."

"It was after Gretchen sold the farm." Mark thought for a moment. "John Box had stopped raising mink a few years before he died due to ill health. That must have been 1949 or '50. The people who bought the property from Gretchen decided they wanted to make it a fox farm."

"Why would you want to raise fox - foxes? What is the plural for fox?"

"I believe it is foxes. Watch your step," he said pointing to a large muddy area in front of them.

"Thanks."

"You raise them for their pelts, of course. There are still fox farms in the United States and Canada has quite a few."

"I can't believe women still wear fur coats," Samantha commented.

"It's their choice, I guess. Anyway, one night the building caught on fire. The fire department was called but by the time they arrived, the fire was so intense they knew they couldn't save it. All they could do was watch it burn out while making sure it didn't spread to the other buildings. I heard there were over a thousand foxes caged up in there. Maybe, more. People said that you could hear them screaming for miles. Although, I'm sure that's an exaggeration." Mark looked away. "Sorry, this always gets to me.

"That's horrible," Samantha said.

"My father was a volunteer fireman at that time. I remember him telling me that he had nightmares for months after that."

"I gather the owner didn't rebuild?"

"Nope, and I have to tell you that the people living around here couldn't have been happier. Mink and fox farms smell. I mean super bad, especially in the summer when it's hot. So, except for the owner of the fox farm, no one was sad about that building burning down."

"How did the fire start?"

"No one knows for sure. It was speculated that it was arson, but that was never proved." He pushed on a door and slid it out of the way, "Shall we?"

Samantha walked into the small barn and looked around. She was surprised to see a half-wall dividing the building. She looked at Mark with a puzzled look on her face. "Why the separation?"

"Horses and pigs don't get along well. Pigs can be mean and horses can get skittish around them. So, they made sure the pigs couldn't get to the horses."

"I thought pigs spent most of their lives outside rolling around in the mud."

Mark smiled. "They do, except when the ground is frozen. The fence around the sty fell apart years ago. There was no reason to repair it as *no one had pigs after John Box*," he said emphatically.

Samantha grinned. "Okay, I heard you. No pigs here for years. The barn isn't in horrible shape, but I don't see any reason why I should keep it."

"You could have horses if you buy the property. Do you ride?"

Samantha smiled. "I'm afraid not. Let's take a quick look at the inside of the garage and that other small building. A tool shed, right?"

"Right. Although, the tool shed should probably be razed for sure. It's in bad shape and the last time I opened the door I was stung by a wasp. I'm pretty sure there's a whole bunch of nests in there."

"I'll pass on that one."

"The garage is in pretty good shape for its age. I believe it was built in 1960 or thereabout. It needs some paint, of course. But, it is heated, which is a plus. We have some pretty cold winters here and it's always nice when it's ten below zero and your car starts."

"I'm anxious to see the inside again," Samantha said as she waited for Mark to open the front door.

Mark unlocked the door and swung it open. "After you."

Samantha didn't move. "Would you mind giving me a few minutes alone?"

"You don't want to go inside?"

Samantha smiled. "No, it's not that. I know this may sound strange but I'd like a few minutes alone inside."

"Oh. That's fine," Mark said, looking confused. "Go ahead."

"Thanks," Samantha said as she brushed past him and entered the house. She turned to Mark. "Please shut the door."

(1942)

John Box held his daughter as she wept. He had known when he saw the car pull up and two military men walk to the house, that bad news was on his doorstep.

Luke was dead the men told Gretchen, killed in action in Germany. Gretchen, who was holding Sarah, handed the baby to her mother. "Father..." was all she said before she collapsed onto the floor.

"It's my fault," Martha told John as she rubbed a cold wet cloth on Gretchen's forehead. "God is punishing us for what I did."

John picked up a bible that was on a small table next to the davenport and opened it. As he started to read out loud, tears welled up in his eyes. He rubbed them away with the back of his hand. "God is a merciful God. He will not slumber or sleep..." He let the book fall from his hands and started to cry.

"At least Luke will be brought home and we can give him a decent funeral," Martha said quietly, as the tears rolled down her cheeks. "He will be laid to rest next to his brother."

John fell to his knees, sobbing loudly. "Dear God, how much more must we suffer? Haven't you done enough to punish us? At least spare my daughter any more agony. She, who did nothing wrong, has been punished enough," he pleaded. He reached out for Martha to take his hand. She went to him, knelt beside him, and together they prayed.

Samantha stood in the kitchen of the old house, a chill running down her spine. She walked into the living room and looked around. "Gretchen, how did you ever manage to survive?" she whispered.

She turned and walked to the door and opened it. "Come on in," she told Mark.

"Are you okay?"

"I'm fine," she said smiling. "I want to check this house out again from top to bottom. Can you turn on the breaker for the elevator? I want to see if it works."

Chapter Seven

Samantha and Mark exited the elevator. "Well, at least that works," Samantha exclaimed happily.

"Yeah, but it's a little shaky," Mark commented. "I'd have it examined by an elevator company if you plan on using it."

"I will," Samantha said. "If I buy the house," she added, smiling. "I gather the elevator was put in by the same gentleman who put so much work and money into the house."

"He planned for everything. This house has a lot of steps. I guess he figured it would be easier to use an elevator instead of climbing up and down stairs when you got old."

"You're guessing, aren't you? You don't know why he put in this elevator."

"You got me," Mark replied. "I haven't a clue."

"Do you always make up stories when you're trying to sell a house?" Samantha asked him.

"Only when I have to," he told her grinning.

"I'm beginning to wonder if anything you've told me is the truth."

"Almost everything is," he said.

Samantha smiled. "Good to know. Now, if we can be serious for a moment, I have something to ask you."

"Of course."

"As you have probably gathered, I'm seriously considering putting an offer on the house. There's one thing, though, that I'd like to do first. I'm aware that after an offer is accepted you only have so many days for a home inspection, a lawyer's approval of the contract, and so on. Do you think it would be possible for me to have a home inspection before I make an offer?"

"I'm not sure how the owner would feel about that. It would be a little unusual."

"Can you contact him and ask?"

"I suppose, but why the rush for the inspection?"

"It's a time thing. If I could have the inspection done now, while I'm in town, I could wrap everything up while I'm here. If I decide to buy it, of course. I'd rather stay in town a few more days than have to travel back and forth for every little thing."

Mark hesitated, thinking.

"Maybe, I should talk to the owner and ask him, if that would be easier for you," Samantha suggested.

"The property is in a trust. I'm not at liberty to tell you who the house belongs to."

"I see," she said, looking disappointed.

"However, seeing as how I'm the trustee of the trust, I guess I could allow it."

"You could have told me that up front."

Mark shrugged. "Sorry, but I had to consider it for a moment. You know, make sure I wasn't breaking any rules."

"So, it's okay, then?"

"I don't see any reason why not."

"Great. Is it okay to set it up for tomorrow?"

"You are moving fast. However, I think tomorrow will be fine."

"Good." Samantha stepped away from the elevator and walked towards one of the bedrooms.

"This place is so much bigger than it looks from

the outside, isn't it?"

"It is deceiving."

"Which room was Sarah's? Do you know?"

"I believe Gretchen and Sarah had the two bedrooms on this floor after they moved back in."

"And, the boys, Luke and Zeke? Which floor were they on?"

Mark gave her a strange look. "I thought I..."

"What?"

"The boys never lived here. Well, Luke did when he was just a baby, but Gretchen and Ray moved across the road before Zeke was born. That's where the boys grew up."

"I missed something. Why didn't Zeke live here? I thought he... After Ray was killed, didn't..." She looked at him confused. "What did I miss?"

"Zeke died when he was seventeen years old," Mark told her.

(1941)

"Who could that be? Are you expecting anyone?" Gretchen asked her mother.

"No, and It's kind of late for a visitor," Martha said, as she walked to the door and opened it.

"Officer Roberts," she said, looking surprised. *"We were just about to turn in. Do you have news about Ray?"*

"May I come in?" he asked.

"Of course."

"Mother? What is it?" Samantha asked, getting off the couch as her mother and the police officer approached her. *"Did they find Ray?"*

"I'm not sure," Martha replied. "Please sit down. May I get you something to drink?

Officer Roberts stayed where he was, fidgeting as he held his hat in his hands. "No thank you, ma'am." He looked at the floor for a moment, obviously uncomfortable.

"What is it?" Martha inquired, getting concerned over the way he was acting.

"I'm sorry to inform you that there's been an accident."

"Is it Ray?" Gretchen exclaimed. "Is he okay?" she asked innocently.

He hesitated. "No, I still don't have any news about Ray. However..." He looked at her. "I'm sorry, Gretchen, but your son, Zeke, has been killed in a hunting accident," he blurted out.

Gretchen stared at him. "No. It can't be. You're wrong."

"I'm so sorry," Roberts said.

"Noo!" she cried out. "It can't be him. It has to be a mistake. Please..." She fell back onto the couch. "Please, not Zeke."

Martha sat down, never taking her eyes off of Roberts. "How could such a thing happen? I can't believe this."

"It seems him and his grandpa went off in different directions in the woods and well..."

"Mother, he said Zeke is dead," Gretchen exclaimed interrupting the policeman. "Tell him he's wrong," she said sobbing. "He's wrong. Do something," she pleaded. "Please, Mother..." Her voice trailed off as her crying escalated.

Martha took her hand. "I'm so sorry, Gretchen." She pulled her daughter close to her and hugged her. The tears rolled down her cheeks as she looked up at Officer Roberts. "You *said a hunting accident. Was he shot?"*

Officer Roberts shook his head yes. "I'm sorry."

"How do you know this?"

"I received a call from the Spooner police department. They asked me to notify you."

"I see. What about John? Where is he?"

"John is making arrangements to bring Zeke home. He won't be charged, of course. It was just a horrible accident."

"What do you mean, he won't be charged? Why would he be charged?" Gretchen asked, crying so hard she was barely able to get the words out.

"I'm sorry, Gretchen. John mistook Zeke for a deer. It was his shot that killed him."

As the news sunk in, Martha's face turned white. "No!" she cried out. "You're lying." She reached out to Roberts, her head spinning as everything went black.

Samantha stared at Mark, shocked. "You must be kidding. John Box killed his own grandson?"

"It was probably one of the saddest things this town ever went through. John Box was a good man and well-liked by everyone who knew him. He was never the same after that. Of course, with Zeke being killed only a couple of days after his father went missing, no one bothered about Ray anymore."

"This is too much," Samantha said. "How could Gretchen not lose her mind? Her mother kills her husband and she loses her youngest son a couple of days later. And, then, on top of that, a few months after she has a baby she gets word that her oldest son has been killed in Germany. How could any one person be sane after that?"

"It certainly was a lot to deal with," Mark agreed.

"I get the feeling this house may be cursed," Samantha declared.

"Yeah, right," Mark said laughing nervously. "You don't believe in that stuff, do you?"

"I think I'm beginning to since I've been around you. This house has seen more than its share of trouble."

"So, it seems. But, you have to remember that all this took place over a lot of years."

Samantha walked over to a window and looked out at the property. "It's all good," she told Mark, after a few moments. "I'm not getting any bad vibes from this house."

"I'm glad to hear it."

"The floors will all have to be refinished. Do you have people in town that can do that? I'll need recommendations for painters, too. And, house cleaners. Is there someone in town that you hire to clean this place? It needs a thorough cleaning?"

Mark smiled, glad she was off the subject of a curse. "I know someone."

"Good. You're paying for that, of course," she stated.

"I am?"

"Well, I mean the trust should pay, don't you think? You should have had it cleaned before you put it on the market and started showing it to people."

"I'm not exactly..." he stopped as Samantha frowned.

"Right. The cost of a good cleaning will come out

of the trust."

"Good." She walked over to a window and looked out. "I'll need to rent a bulldozer," Samantha exclaimed. "I want to tear down the toolshed and that old barn. I'm going to put sod down and have flower beds and..." She stopped talking and looked at Mark, who was grinning from ear to ear. "What?"

"It sounds like you're buying a house."

Samantha laughed. "It does, doesn't it? Well, I guess it all depends on what the home inspection shows. What time is good for you tomorrow? You know, to let him into the house."

"I'll work with you. You tell me."

"I'll give Toots a call and set it up. I'll let you know."

"Toots?"

"It's a nickname. His name is Sven Petersen. He's going to do the inspection. I'll call you after I talk to him."

"Sounds good."

"Do you have an appliance store in town?"

"Not really. If you want a good selection of appliances, you'll need to go to Beaver Dam, Sun Prairie, or Madison."

Samantha grinned. "Ok, so no appliance store in town. Should we take the elevator down to the next floor or do you want to walk?"

Chapter Eight

"What are you doing for dinner tonight?" Mark asked Samantha as they drove away from the house.

Samantha glanced over at him. "No plans. Why?"

"I was wondering if you are free for dinner."

She smiled. "I am."

"Would you like to have dinner with me?"

"I'd love to."

"Great," Mark replied. "How does six-thirty sound?"

"Sounds good to me."

"I'll pick you up in front of the motel."

"You don't have to pick me up. Columbus is a small town. I'm sure I'll be able to find your house."

Mark glanced over at her. "My house? Why would you come to my house?"

She looked confused. "Didn't you just ask me to have dinner with you and your family?"

Mark smiled. "No. Just with me and I'm not cooking, Samantha. I don't want to kill you off. At least, not before you buy a house from me."

"I'm sorry. I thought you were asking me to join you and your family for dinner. Exactly what did..." She laughed. "How about we start over?"

"We're here," Mark commented as he pulled into a parking spot in front of his office. He turned off the car and looked at Samantha. "I would like to take you out for dinner. At a restaurant."

"And, your wife won't mind?"

Mark laughed. "So that's it. I'm not married,

41

Samantha. I was once but not anymore. Sorry, but it will just be you and me."

"Oh, no. That's fine. It's just that I thought that was a wedding band on your finger."

"Well, it is but it's not mine. It was my dad's. I've worn it since he died. It makes me feel close to him," he told her smiling. "Anyway, I just thought you might like a good steak dinner. No strings attached. Just a realtor taking his client out for a meal."

"Of course, I'd love to join you for dinner. Sixty-thirty it is."

"Just a heads up," Mark said as Samantha opened the car door. "We're not fancy here in town, so dress casually."

"Will do," she replied as she exited Mark's car. "See you later."

Mark watched her walk to her car, get in, and drive away. He sighed as he got out of his car and walked into his office. "Any messages?" he asked his office manager, Gloria.

"Nope. Well, did she buy it?" the manager asked.

"No. She wants an inspection before she puts in an offer."

"That's a little unusual, isn't it?" Gloria asked. What did you tell her?"

"That it was fine. At this point, I'd do anything to sell that place. She's setting up the inspection for tomorrow."

"That soon? What's the rush?"

"I have no idea, but if an inspection tomorrow is what it takes for her to buy that place, I'm all for it. And, before you hear it from the town gossips, I'm taking her to dinner tonight. Strictly business."

"Really? Going to turn on that Starckweather charm, are you?"

"Don't start, Gloria."

"I'm not. How much does she know about that place? Are you going to tell her about all the bad shit that went down in that house?"

"Hell, no," he said as he walked towards his office. "Well, maybe some of it." He turned and looked at her. "There have been a lot of people who lived in that house. I don't know if I even remember them all."

"Are you gonna tell her about the murders that took place there?" Gloria asked, grinning. "What about that gangster that lived there?"

"Carlos Moretti? I guess it will depend on how much time I've got and how much I've had to drink. Besides, there's not that much to tell."

"Are you kidding? That house has more history than... I don't know what. Anyway, just behave yourself. You don't want to blow this deal."

"I don't need you to tell me to behave, Gloria."

"Just sell the damn place, will you? I need a paycheck."

Samantha stepped out of the shower, grabbed a towel, and dried herself. She glanced in the mirror at her naked body and smiled. Not bad for an old broad of forty-eight, she thought. She checked the time and decided she had time for a little nap before she had to get ready for dinner. She threw on a terrycloth robe, turned the TV channel to a rerun of Cheers, and curled up on the bed.

Just as she started to drift off, her phone rang. She looked at the caller ID and smiled. "Toots," she answered. "Thanks for calling me back. I have a favor to ask."

"Anything for you, Sam. You know that. So, what can I do you for?"

"I found the house I told you about and I'd like you to take a look at it. Can you do it tomorrow?"

"The one that Moretti used to own in... Wait, don't tell me." He thought for a moment. "Columbus," he declared. "I don't know why I have trouble remembering the name of that town."

"Probably 'cause you're getting old."

"Watch it, girlie. Anyway, I'm in Rockford. How far is that from you?"

"Not far. Probably a little over an hour. What are you doing in Rockford?"

"Joyce's niece had a baby. We drove up to spend a few days with Joyce's sister and to see the little guy. He's cute as a button."

"If I'm not mistaken, that makes you a great-uncle. Congratulations. How is everyone doing?"

"Everyone's fine. The baby is nice and healthy."

"I'm glad to hear it. What did they name him?"

"Atticus."

"Like in Atticus Finch?"

"Yep."

"Poor kid."

"Don't get me started. Now, Sam, what about this house you want me to look at? Big? Little? Attic? Basement? What are we looking at?"

"It's a weird-looking house. I can guarantee you've never seen one like this before. Four stories, four bedrooms, and – get this – it has an elevator."

"No shit! You don't see that every day," Toots told

her.

"I'm gonna buy it. I'm serious about this, Toots. But I need to go through all the motions so no one gets suspicious. And, besides, if you give it a good going over, maybe you can give me some ideas of where to look."

"I'll do my best to help. What time do you want me there?"

"Can you be here around nine? I'll text you the directions."

"Nine works for me. I'll see you tomorrow. And, Sam?"

"Yes?"

"Are you positive you want to do this?"

"Absolutely."

"You understand that it may be a big waste of time and money, don't you?"

"I know. But, what if it really is here? I have to find out, Toots. Plus... Well, you know."

"I know, kiddo. I'll do whatever I can do to help..." He paused. "You know I'll always be here for you."

"I know. Thanks, Toots. I love you."

Chapter Nine

"Did you get in touch with *Toots*?" Mark asked Samantha, grinning.

"You wouldn't be grinning like that if he was sitting here," she told him. "And, yes, I talked to him. He will be here around nine tomorrow morning."

"So, is this his full-time job? I know a few guys who work full time and do home inspections on the side."

Samantha looked up from her plate. "This is an excellent steak," she commented. "Do you come here often?"

"If you want a good steak, you can't beat Club 60. I used to frequent the Capri, which was right downtown but it closed a while back." He watched her take another mouthful and grinned. "I'm glad you're enjoying it."

"Toots isn't a home inspector. He's a builder – a contractor. He knows everything," Samantha told him, referring back to the previous subject.

Mark laughed. "Everything is a lot to know."

"And, he knows it. He's been in the business for a long time, Mark. Plus, he's an old friend of the family. He's like an uncle to me. I'd trust him with my life."

"I'm anxious to meet him."

"Is there anything else I should know about that house? You said it wasn't cursed, but are there any ghosts and goblins hanging around that I should know about?"

"We have a few houses around here that could be haunted. There's a big house on Ludington Street that people say was haunted years ago. However, I've never heard of any ghosts hanging around out at the Box House."

"Good to know. I guess I won't have to sleep with the lights on." She finished off her steak and wiped her mouth with her napkin. "Who else lived there?"

"You mean after Gretchen sold it and moved away?"

"Uh-huh."

"Well, let's see," Mark said, thinking about what to tell her. "After John died in 1947, Gretchen and Sarah continued to live in the house with Martha. Martha passed on in 1949 and Gretchen immediately put the property up for sale. It sold fast and the couple who bought it stayed there until..." He thought for a moment. "I believe they stayed there until the Kingsford family bought it in 1960."

"They were the rich people who fixed it up. Right?"

"Right. Nicholas Kingsford – he was a third, by the way - had money to burn. Why he ever decided on buying that place – well, I don't get it. There were a lot of homes in better shape for sale in Columbus. Although..."

"What?"

"I remember someone telling me that his daughter loved to ride so maybe that's the reason. There was a barn there already, which would have been perfect for a couple of horses." He shrugged. "Who knows? Anyway, he brought in workers from Chicago and Milwaukee and remodeled the entire inside. The company that put in the elevator came all the way from New York. The wood floors were torn up and replaced with Brazilian Cherry and Hickory. He had carpenters add crown molding in most of the rooms."

"Some of the floors are in bad shape. I can't wait to see what they will look like after they are refinished."

Mark grinned. "You are so going to buy that house."

"We'll see," Samantha replied.

"How about those bathrooms? Most older homes only have one bathroom but this house has one on each floor. You can't beat that for convenience."

"I did find that interesting, but I guess if you're going to remodel and can afford it, you might as well go whole hog," Samantha said.

"He spent close to three years redoing that house. Plus, he built the garage. It's even heated."

"I know. You told me already."

"Sorry. I didn't mean to repeat myself."

"Why didn't Kingsford move in after the renovations were completed?" she asked.

"Kingsford never had any intentions of moving into that house."

"What?" Samantha asked, surprised. "What do you mean; he never intended to live there?"

"It was meant to be a wedding gift for his daughter and future son-in-law."

Samantha sat back in her chair and stared at Mark. "You're going to make me ask, aren't you?"

Mark grinned. "Her name was Margaret and she grew up in Milwaukee. After she graduated from high school, she got a job in Madison. She met a nice young man from town and after they dated for about a year, he asked her to marry him. She said yes and they agreed to wait until she was twenty-one. They figured it would give her fiancé a chance to get established in business here in town."

"Here? He lived in Columbus?"

"Right." Mark took a sip of water. "It also gave her father the time he needed to fix up the house. I guess that was one of the reasons it took so long. He knew he had time before the wedding, so he didn't push the people working on the house."

"All right," Samantha said. "I see where this is going."

"Where do you think it's going?" Mark asked.

"They both died in a horrible car accident or plane crash or something like that."

"Wrong."

"The plague, then."

Mark smiled. "Nope. One night, a few weeks before the wedding, Margaret was at a party in Madison with a bunch of friends. She got drunk and one of the guys at the party raped her. Now, hard as it might be to believe that there were any virgins left in the '60s, Margaret was one and proud of it. Thinking that her fiancé would no longer want her, she wrote a suicide note, filled her bathtub with water, crawled into it, and slit her wrists."

"Are you serious? Who would kill herself just because she's no longer a virgin?"

"Well, obviously, Margaret Kingsford. However, you need to remember that she was extremely distraught from being raped. According to the note she left, that was why she thought her fiancé would no longer want to marry her."

"Sorry, I didn't mean to sound unsympathetic. What happened to her fiancé after she killed herself? Do I dare to ask?"

"When he received the news that Margaret was dead, he went down to the train station and waited for the next train to show up. Well, the next train happened to be a freight train..."

"And, he stepped in front of it and killed himself," Samantha interrupted. "Right?"

Mark sat back and frowned. "Nice way to kill an ending."

"But, I was right. Right?"

Mark just stared at her.

"Right?" Samantha asked again, louder this time.

"Yes, you're right. Are you ready to leave or do you want more coffee?"

"I'm finished. It was a great meal. Thank you."

"Did you hear that story before?" he asked, as they walked out of the restaurant.

"What story would that be?"

"About Margaret."

"Nope. First time."

"How did you know it would end tragically?"

"It was just a guess. After hearing the other stories you've been telling me about that house, I figured something horrible had to have happened."

Mark drove past the hospital and down Park Avenue. As they reached the center of town, he glanced over at Samantha. "Do you want to stop for a nightcap before you go back to the motel?"

Samantha hesitated for a moment. "It's tempting, but tomorrow's going to be a busy day. I think I should call it a night."

"Sure thing," Mark said as he made a left at the

stoplight.

"Do you live in town, Mark?"

"I do. In fact, it's only a few blocks that way," he said, pointing to his left as they passed by Lewis Street. "It's nothing fancy but it's home."

"I'm sure it's very nice," Samantha replied.

"Would you like to see it?" Mark asked, slowing down a little. "I could put on a pot of coffee."

"It's tempting, but no. Maybe, I could have a rain check?"

"Absolutely."

"Mark, I'm curious about something."

"What's that?"

"How do you know so much about that house?"

Mark smiled. "Columbus is a small town, Samantha. Everybody who lives here knows everything about everybody. I was born here. So were my father and my grandfather. I've heard stories about that house since I can remember." He caught the green light and turned onto Industrial Drive. "Here's your temporary home," he told her as he pulled into the motel's parking lot.

"Then, you know who lived there after the Kingsford family sold it."

"Of course."

Samantha glanced over at him. "I'd like to hear about them. How about you come in for a few minutes and continue this story?"

"I thought you were tired?"

"I am, but hearing about this house fascinates me. The motel has a sitting area. We could talk in there."

"I guess, but only for a few minutes."

51

"Great." She looked around and smiled. "You lucked out. There's a parking spot right there in front of the motel."

"After his daughter died, Kingsford let the house sit empty until around 1975. He paid the taxes every year and he made sure the lawn was mowed during the summer. But, that was all he did. He died in the fall of 1975 and his wife put the property up for sale. No one bought it, so she turned it over to my father and asked him to see if he could rent it."

"Your father?"

"My father owned Starckweather Realty and, at that time, they handled most of the rental properties in town."

"I gather you own it now," Samantha declared.

"I do. I took over after dad quit working. Anyway, there were quite a few different families who lived in that house. Most of them didn't stay very long." He laughed.

"What's funny?"

"With so many people moving in and out, it started to be called the house with the revolving door. I remember one renter in particular. I believe he moved in around 1979."

Chapter Ten

(1979)

"It's almost two o'clock," Mrs. Albrecht exclaimed. "Where have you been?"

"Elsie, Elsie, Elsie. How many times do I have to explain to you that when my flock needs tending to, time is of no importance?"

"And, just who in your flock needed tending to until two o'clock this morning?"

Rev. Kurt Albrecht ignored her question and walked away from her. "I'm hungry. Is there any of that sauerbraten left from last night?"

"Who was it, Kurt?" she asked again.

"I was with Mr. Gardner, if you must know. He died, Elsie. The poor man passed away while I sat beside his death bed and prayed with him. I witnessed his death and it was a joyous occasion, for he has left this cruel world and he is with God. Now, I'm hungry and I want something to eat."

"Mr. Gardner died? I didn't know he was ill. I'm sorry I was upset. I'll call Mrs. Gardner tomorrow to see if there is anything she needs," Elsie said. "I'll fix you a plate." As she walked by him to go to the kitchen, she glanced up at him. "Really, I am sorry that I was upset with you, Kurt."

"You have to learn to stop imagining things."

She stared at his neck for a moment. "What is that? Is that blood?"

He put his hand up to his neck and rubbed it. "I'm not sure."

"It looks like lipstick," Elsie declared, reaching out to touch her husband's neck.

Kurt pushed her hand away. "What do you think you're doing?" he yelled.

"It is lipstick," Elsie cried out. "You have been with another woman. I knew it."

"You're crazy. You're imagining things."

"Did Mr. Gardner die or is that another one of your ridiculous lies?"

"Of course, he died!" Reverend Albrecht shouted. "I would never make something like that up. What's wrong with you, woman?"

"And, then what? While her husband lay on his death bed, did you comfort her?"

Reverend Albrecht "Of course, I did. The woman was devastated. Her husband was dying. She cried and I comforted her."

"How? By having sex with her?"

"I did what had to be done in her time of need," he replied. "She needed me and I was there for her."

"You promised me it would never happen again," Elsie yelled as she slapped Kurt in the face. "You're a pig. I hate you."

Kurt put his hand to his face, shocked that his wife would dare to hit him. "You will pay for that," he said angrily, as he grabbed her arm and pulled her towards him. "Take off your underwear."

"No, please. I'm sorry I hit you," Elsie cried out, tears

54

filling her eyes.

"Off! Now! Or, I'll rip them off of you."

Still crying, Elsie reached under her nightgown and pulled down her panties.

Kurt watched, smirking cruelly. "Good. Now, over my knees."

Elsie backed away from him. "No," she said stubbornly. "Leave me alone."

Kurt reached out, dug his fingers into her arm, and pulled her onto his lap. He lifted her nightgown, exposing her bare bottom. He rubbed it gently for a few moments. "So nice," he murmured. Then, using the flat of his hand, he struck her.

"Please, stop," Elsie cried out. "I'm sorry."

"But, I'm not done. We always do ten. Remember?" he reminded her as he continued to spank her. "Three, two, one. There, now we're done." He pushed her off his lap onto the floor and smiled.

She looked up at him, still crying. "That hurt."

"It was supposed to hurt, Elsie. Now, have you learned your lesson?" Kurt asked her.

"Yes."

"And, are you going to ever strike me again?"

"No."

"What are you going to do now?"

"Please, Kurt, I don't want to."

"You have to. You know that it's part of the lesson. How else are you going to learn," Kurt said, as he unzipped his trousers.

55

Samantha looked Mark in the eyes and frowned. "I don't believe you. You're lying again. You made that whole story up, didn't you?"

Mark grinned. "You would think so, wouldn't you? However, it's true."

Samantha shook her head. "I doubt it."

"Should I stop?"

Samantha hesitated. "Not yet. I mean, if it's really true, I want to know what happened."

"It seems that the spankings became more and more frequent. So, one night, when Reverend Albrecht arrived home sometime after midnight, Elsie was waiting behind the door. As he came strolling into the house, Elsie hit him in the head with a cast-iron frying pan, knocking him out."

"She didn't kill him?"

"Well, she kinda did. It wasn't the first blow that did it, but the coroner determined that it could have been any one of the seven or eight that followed."

Samantha studied Mark's face, trying to determine if he was pulling her leg. "You're serious, aren't you?" she finally asked.

"I am. If you have any doubts, you might want to visit the library one day and check it out for yourself. You'll find everything I've just told you in the newspapers from back then.

"I might just do that, but I doubt the story of the Reverend spanking his wife is in the newspapers."

"Some of it is. It all came out during the trial. She sat on the stand and told the judge and the jury exactly how her husband abused her."

Samantha grinned. "Actually, it's kind of kinky, isn't it? I mean, pulling her pants down and getting

56

spanked. Well, it's not something you hear about every day."

"You're right. Usually, it's a porn flick where little teen-age school girls are being spanked by their principal for being naughty girls."

"Well, I imagine you know more about that than I do," Samantha said grinning. "I'm not really into porn." She stood up and started to pace back and forth. "You've told me some pretty weird stories about that house. I'm beginning to think I should pack up and get the hell out of Dodge. That house may not be haunted but it sure as hell sounds like it's cursed."

"Nah. It's not cursed. It's just been lived in by a lot of people who have had a lot of bad luck."

"You think?" She sat back down and sighed. "So, what happened to Elsie?"

"They charged her with the accidental death of her husband. The jury found her guilty and she was sentenced to six months in jail."

"Accidental death? You're kidding."

"She never spent a day in jail after the trial. Her attorney showed the jury pictures of her rear end all bruised from being hit. And, except for one man, the jury was all women. She got off with time served."

"When did all this happen?"

"They moved into the house in 1979. They lived there for quite a while. Longer than most of the renters. I think it was around five years." He thought for a few moments and smiled. "Yeah, Elsie killed him in 1984. I was a freshman in high school at the time. It was the talk of the town. I mean, how many times do you hear about a minister cheating on his wife, much less her killing him for it? It was big news at the time. Even the

Milwaukee Journal sent out reporters to cover the story."

"What happened to the house after that? Were there more renters?"

"A few, but the house was probably empty more than lived in after that. Mrs. Kingsford died and the house went to a nephew who had no interest in it at all. Once again, the house was put up for sale, and, once again, there were no takers. We kept the house on the market and continued to rent it out until 2000, when we finally got a buyer. Mark glanced at his watch. "I should go."

"Wait. Who bought the house?" She inquired.

"I should leave, Samantha. You need your rest. You have a big day tomorrow."

"I guess." She smiled at him. "Are you still up for a nightcap?" Samantha asked suddenly.

"Now?" Mark asked, surprised at the invitation. "It's a little late, don't you think?"

"I have a bottle in my room. All we need is a little ice and a couple of glasses. How about it?"

Mark held back a grin. "I'm not sure if that is a good idea."

"It's just one drink. What can it hurt?" Samantha said.

"One drink and that's it," Mark stated.

"That's fine." She waited while Mark got up from his chair. "So, tell me about those rich people," she said smiling, as they walked out of the sitting room and headed towards the elevator.

"Have you ever heard of Carlos Moretti?" Mark asked her as he pushed the button for the second floor.

Chapter Eleven

(2000)

Columbus didn't change much over the years. By the year 2000, a few new businesses had opened and some old ones had closed. River Road still flooded during heavy rains and was occasionally closed to traffic. The Box House had been empty for years. Starckweather Realty's FOR SALE sign leaned so far that it was touching the ground and the grass-covered all but the top. And, much to the relief of the world's population, they had survived the millennium.

Carlos Moretti parked his Lincoln Continental on the side of the road and stared at the weird-looking house. "That shit box has to be the ugliest house I've ever seen," he remarked.

"The grass needs cutting," Tony Rossi commented. "The garage is nice, though," he added.

"The paint is peeling. It's a mess. Everything needs to be painted," Carlos complained.

"That ain't a big deal, Boss. Anyway, what difference does it make? It ain't like you're gonna live here or anything."

"I might sometimes. Besides, I've got a reputation to uphold. I can't have these people thinking I'm too cheap to fix up a house."

Tony glanced at his watch. "Shouldn't that Mark guy be here by now? It's almost eleven."

"I told him eleven." Tony turned his head as a car slowed down and drove onto the property. "That's him now. Right on *time. I like that in a person."*

"You think you're gonna buy this dump?" Tony asked, as Carlos started his car, drove up the small incline onto the property, and parked behind Mark's car.

"If the price is right." He grinned. "Maybe, I'll make him an offer he can't refuse," he said, laughing loudly.

Tony laughed. "Good one, Boss."

Two hours later, Carlos Moretti made an offer on the property.

"That's a pretty low offer," Mark told Carlos. "I'm not sure the owner will consider it."

"You won't know if you don't ask. I'm not trying to insult the guy or anything, but there's a lot of work that needs to be done here. You know, to fix it up and make it look decent. So, give him a call."

"Give me a minute," Mark said. He walked over to his car and opened the door. He sat down and made a phone call.

"Do you think the guy will go for it?" Tony asked Carlos.

Carlos shrugged. "How the fuck should I know." He kept his eyes focused on Mark, waiting for him to hang up.

"He's coming back," Tony said as he poked Carlos on the arm.

"Will you stop that?"

"My seller was wondering if you could go up a little," Mark told Carlos.

"How much is a little?"

"Another five."

Carlos stared at Mark. "Five?" He thought for a minute. "Ah, what the hell's another five thousand? You got yourself a deal but you gotta get somebody out here to cut this grass."

Mark smiled. "Congratulations, and thank you. I'll have the yard taken care of as soon as possible."

"What do I have to sign?" Carlos asked.

"Just the usual contract. This is a cash deal, so it won't be too involved. I imagine you'll want a lawyer's approval and a home inspection."

Carlos shook his head. "Nah, I'll take it as is. I don't need all that inspection and lawyer shit."

"Really?" Mark said, surprised. "Are you sure?"

"I saw enough."

"Well, if you're sure. How much will you be putting into escrow?"

Carlos reached into his pocket and pulled out a wad of bills. He counted off $5,000.00 in hundreds and handed it to Mark. "Here's five grand. Is that enough?"

"It certainly is." He laid his briefcase on the hood of his car and opened it. "I'll just write out a receipt for that," he told Carlos as he carefully tucked the money into a pocket in the cover of the briefcase.

"I don't need no receipt. I trust you," Carlos told him. "We gotta get back to Chicago. How long will it take you to get the papers ready?"

"I'll need about an hour or so. It's a cash deal and you're declining all the contingencies, so it's pretty routine. How does that fit into your schedule?"

"Are you hungry?" Carlos asked, looking a Tony.

"I'm always hungry. You know that."

"We're gonna go get something to eat. We'll meet you back at your office in an hour or so. We can sign the papers then."

"Sounds good." Mark waited until Carlos and Tony got into the Lincoln and drove away. He pulled his phone out of his pocket and hit a number. "Hey, Dad," he exclaimed, grinning. "He bought it."

"I want two of yous guys here all the time," Carlos informed the men sitting around the kitchen table. "This place has to look lived in and the outside can't be overrun with weeds and shit." He looked at the six men and grinned. "Any volunteers?"

No one said a word.

"I didn't think so." He looked at one of the men. "Rosey, you find me someone to live here and take care of this place."

Rosey glanced over Gino. "What about your nephew and his wife? He lived on a farm once. Is he out of the slammer yet?"

"He's been out about two months now," Gino told him.

"What's he doing? Is he working or something?" Carlos inquired.

Gino grinned. "I don't know, but he should be able to cut the grass and pull a few weeds. I let him know he's got a new job."

"That's settled then. Your nephew can take care of the outside and his wife can take care of the inside. You tell your nephew to buy himself a couple of pairs of nice overalls and some work boots. It's on me," Carlos said.

Tony grinned. "That's nice of you, Boss."

"Now, one more thing..." Carlos stared at the six men, making them feel uncomfortable.

"Boss?" Tony finally said, after a few moments.

He held up his hand. "Just wait." He looked away thinking. "Yous guys don't bring nobody out here unless it's sanctioned by me. You don't tell nobody about this place, either. Understood?" He waited as the men mumbled that they understood. "Good."

"Anything else, Boss?" Tony asked as he stood up.

Carlos shot him a dirty look. "Do I look like I'm done talking? Sit your ass down."

"Sorry," Tony muttered as he sat down.

"One last thing I got to say," Carlos told the men. "Except for Gino's nephew and his wife, you stay out of town. No going anyplace when you're here. We don't want nobody recognizing you from the papers or shit. If you need something, you tell Gino's nephew..." He looked over at Gino. "What the hell is your nephew's name anyway?"

"I think it's Frank."

"You think?"

"He changes it all the time, but he was born Frank. I don't know what he's calling himself these days. His wife's name is Kari. She's very quiet. She doesn't talk a lot."

"Maybe, I shoulda married her," Carlos said, grinning. "My old lady don't shut up," he added, laughing.

"Good one, Boss," Tony said, as he and the rest of the men laughed.

"Rosey?"

"Yeah?"

"You walk the property tomorrow. Check the fences to be sure they don't need no fixin'. I don't want nobody around here thinking they can cut across my property. Put up some warning signs, like Keep Off and stuff," Carlos instructed. "We don't need no one watching us digging holes out back." He thought for a moment. "Put up a couple of those Beware of the Dog signs, too," he added.

"Are you getting a dog?" Rosey asked.

"Hell, no, I'm not getting a dog. Just put up some fucking signs, will ya?"

"Sure thing, Carlos."

"Sorry, but I gotta go, Boss," Tony interrupted. "I gotta meet with a couple of guys who owe me some money. Do you need me for anything else?"

"Go. Get outta here. Go do your meet." He took a long sip of iced tea. "Are the rest of yous guys planning to spend the night or what?"

"I'm Tony's ride, so I'm leaving, too," Gino told him. "I'll see you back in town, Carlos."

"All right, then, you two get out of here," Carlos said. He reached into his jacket pocket and pulled out a deck of cards. "The rest of us are gonna be playing a little five-card draw. Ante up, everyone. The name of the game is Carlos wins."

"No way!" Samantha sat back on the bed and shook her head in disbelief. She fished an ice cube out of her glass and put it in her mouth. "You're telling me that Carlos Moretti lived in the house I might buy?"

"Again, I direct you to the town library. Check it out. It's in all the newspapers." Mark emptied his glass and set it down on a table.

"You want another one?" Samantha asked as she chewed up what was left of the piece of ice.

Mark hesitated. "I don't think so. It's late. I should go."

"Well, I'm having another one, so you might as well join me and finish your story."

"You're a bad influence. You know that?"

Samantha grinned. "So, I've been told." She handed him her glass. "More, please."

(2000)

"I'm telling you, Carlos, the kid needs help."

"Tell him to eat some spinach and grow a few."

"The ground out there is hard. It's like trying to shovel through rock. If he uses a backhoe, he'd be able to get to at least six to eight feet. Maybe, deeper."

"Why would we need to go deeper?"

"We don't. But, the deeper we go, the less likely the animals are gonna dig 'em up."

"That's a lot of money, Gino."

"You can pick up a used one pretty cheap. I'll check around and try to find something under ten grand."

"Bullshit! I'm not spending another ten grand on that place."

"How about I pay for it?" Gino asked.

Carlos grinned. "Now, that's an offer I like. You're a good man, Gino, trying to help your nephew. I like you."

"Thanks, Gino. I appreciate that."

"I'll split it with you," Carlos told him, suddenly feeling generous. *"Whatever you can get for ten or under is okay with me."*

Gino smiled. *"I'll get on it. Thanks."*

Chapter Twelve

Samantha opened her eyes and glanced over at Mark.

"There you are. I thought you fell asleep," Mark said.

"I heard every word. Did they get it?"

"Get what?"

"That backhoe thing."

"What do you think they used to dig all those holes?" he said, yawning. "I need to go."

"I'm not sure you should be driving anywhere in your condition. Maybe, I should take you home."

"I see. You don't think I'm in any condition to drive but you think you are. Well, you're not and you're not going anywhere, anywho. So there."

Samantha grinned. "Methinks thou aren't sober any longer."

"Can I sleep here? You've got two beds. Why do you need two beds? There's only one of you. Do you switch and use one one night and the next night..."

"Does this town have Uber?" Samantha asked Mark, interrupting his nonsense.

"I'll drive," Mark declared.

"That's it. I'm taking you home. "Come on." She got off the bed and took Mark's arm. "Let's go," Samantha said, as he pulled away from her and plopped down on the bed. "Shit," she uttered. She thought for a moment, reached down and pulled Mark's shoes off, put a pillow under his head, and turned on the TV.

"Lightweight," she murmured, as she turned off

the light and lowered the volume on the television.

"You know they found six, don't you?" Mark mumbled.

"I thought you passed out."

"Nope, just resting my eyeballs."

"Six what?' Samantha asked after a few seconds of silence.

"Bodies. Out there, scattered all around the field out there in back of that barn out there."

Samantha didn't say anything.

"It's kinda dark in here," Mark declared.

"I turned the light off."

"That must be why it's dark in here. Can I sleep over?"

Samantha sighed. "For a few hours."

"Move over."

Samantha laughed. "Not with me, you idiot. Go to sleep. I'll wake you early so you can get out of here before anyone sees you."

"That's – that's so good of you. I don't want to ruin my fine repro – reprotration."

"Go to sleep."

"Night."

Samantha turned the TV off, grabbed the bedspread, covered herself, and closed her eyes.

"Anyway, by the time the Feds figured out what Moretti was doing – well, you know what?"

"What?" Samantha asked, sighing.

"Those guys, they had already buried at least sixty bodies in that field."

"Sixty, Mark? Really?"

"No. Six. I mean six. Six bodies."

<u>(2005)</u>

"We've covered every inch of that field. I'm comfortable that we've recovered all the bodies," Federal Agent Sam Shepherd told the group of reporters standing just outside the property line.

"How can you be sure?" one of the reporters asked.

"We brought in cadaver dogs and used GPR. I'm confident we found all of them."

"What's GPR?"

"GPR stands for ground-penetrating radar. It's extremely accurate in finding objects located under the surface of the ground."

"How did you find out that Moretti was using this place as a burial ground?"

"We got a tip from a reliable source."

"Can you tell us who?" another reporter shouted out.

"Sorry, that information will not be released at this time. Suffice it to say, we have enough evidence to put Carlos Moretti away for a long time."

"What about the couple that lived here? Did they know what was going on?"

"All we know right now is that they were caretakers, hired by Moretti. There is nothing to suggest that they had anything to do with the murders," Shepherd replied.

"Are you saying that all the bodies had been murdered?"

"I'd like to hold off answering that question until the coroner is finished with his examinations."

"You saw the bodies, Agent. You must have an opinion."

Shepherd hesitated. "I will say that the condition of the bodies when we found them, do indicate that foul play could have been involved."

"So, that's a yes, then," a woman reporter from the Journal stated.

"I didn't say it was a definite. I said could have. Don't put words in my mouth." He looked around the group of reporters. "That's it." He turned to Chief Mitchell. "Chief, do you have anything to add?"

Mitchell, Chief of the Columbus Police Department, stepped in front of the podium. "I believe Agent Shepherd has covered everything that we know to date. We'll keep you informed if there is any additional information that we can share with you. Thank you all for coming. I'd appreciate it if you stay off the property. We are still considering this entire area a crime scene. Thank you."

"Samantha?" Mark listened for a moment. "Are you still awake?"

"Whaat?" she murmured.

"Never mind."

Chapter Thirteen

Sven 'Toots' Petersen drove up the small incline and parked his truck. He glanced around, saw Samantha standing in the yard, and smiled. "There's my girl," he exclaimed as he exited the truck.

Samantha hurried over to him, grinning from ear to ear. "Toots, you're looking as young as ever."

Sven wrapped his arms around her and hugged her, lifting her off the ground a good two feet.

Samantha grunted. "Too hard. You're smothering me," she said laughing.

Sven set her down. "You're a sight for sore eyes, girlie. It's been too long since I've seen you." He looked her up and down. "I see you've acquired a few more gray hairs."

Samantha punched him playfully, "That's not something you're supposed to say to a lady." She turned and looked at the house. "What do you think?"

"This is it, huh? You weren't exaggerating when you said it was strange looking." He turned and looked over the property. "How many acres are there?"

Samantha watched as Mark pulled into the driveway. "I'm not sure. Here's the realtor," she informed Toots.

Mark's jaw dropped a little when he glanced over at Samantha and Toots. "Morning," he called as he got out of his car.

"Good morning," Samantha replied grinning. "How are you feeling this morning?"

Mark shot her a dirty look. "I'll live, no thanks to

you."

"You shouldn't play with the big girls if you can't handle it," she told him, grinning. "Mark, I'd like you to meet Sven Petersen."

"Call me Toots," Sven told him, as he grabbed Mark's hand and shook it. "It's nice to meet you." He glanced down at Samantha. "Sam, do you two have a problem?" Toots asked.

"Nope," Samantha replied, grinning. "I think Mark might have had a little more than he could handle last night."

Toots laughed. "Well, that could mean one of two things or both."

"It's good to meet you," Mark said, ignoring Sven's remark. He looked up at the man. "I'm sorry, I know you must be asked this all the time, but how tall are you?"

Sven smiled. "The last time I was measured, I was six-eleven. I used to be taller but I've shrunk. It seems you get shorter as you get older."

"It happens to all of us, I guess," Mark said. "I bet you played basketball."

"I did, but I wasn't that good at it. Did you play?"

Mark shook his head. "Nah, it wasn't my game. I played a little baseball in school. That's about it." He turned to Samantha. "I'm not staying. You can call me when you're finished and I'll come back and pick up the keys."

"You're leaving? Samantha asked, surprised.

"I am."

"Do you need to go take a nap?" she teased.

"Actually, I do. However, there's no reason to stay. There's nothing for me to do here and I've got a ten o'clock appointment. I'm sure you two can do fine without me." He handed her a key ring with several keys hanging from it. "The keys are marked so you shouldn't have any problem getting into the buildings."

"Okay. I'll call you when we're done."

"See you later," Mark said as he got back in his car.

Samantha smiled at Sven. "It looks like it's all ours. Ready?"

Sven grinned. "Just what did happen last night?"

"Nothing happened, Toots. Mark just can't handle his liquor, that's all."

"He didn't look so good."

"It's kinda my fault. I asked him if he wanted to come up to my room for a drink. He had a little too much and it hit him pretty hard."

"Are you feeling okay?"

Samantha shook her head yes. "I'm fine. I know my limit. Obviously, Mark doesn't."

"Did you serve him that crap you drink?"

"It's not crap. That stuff is expensive."

"I know it wouldn't take much of it to knock out an elephant. And, it doesn't make it better just because it costs more, Sam."

"Well, I like it," she told him.

Toots smiled. "I need to get my tools and I'll be good to go," he told her as he walked towards his truck.

"That's it for me," Samantha told Cindy, their waitress. "What are you gonna have?" Samantha asked Toots.

"I think I'll start with a salad. Russian dressing. I'll have the strip steak, rare, some fries, and... No, make that a baked potato. Lots of sour cream and butter. And, keep the rolls coming. These are great. You make them here?"

"No, sir. We get them from the bakery," Cindy told him, smiling sweetly.

"Well, they sure are tasty."

"Thank you. I'll get your salads."

"So? Do you think there's a chance it could be there?" Samantha asked as she watched Cindy walk away.

"It's a possibility. It's obvious that the barn had a dirt floor when it was built. The cement was added later, a section at a time. I'm surprised the feds didn't tear it up when they searched this place."

"As I understand it, once they found the first body out in the field, they concentrated on that area. Hopefully, that's true."

"The house is in pretty good shape. It could use some updating. However, seeing this is just a fishing expedition, I wouldn't waste my money."

"Okay. What else?"

"There are mice in the house," Sven told her.

"I'll set some traps or get a cat," she replied. "I'm not afraid of a few mice. What about the elevator?"

"What about it?"

"Is it safe, Toots? I don't want to get stuck in it when I'm in that house all alone."

Sven shrugged. "It needs some maintenance, but nothing big as far as I could tell. A little oil would help. Just be sure you have your phone with you when you use it. Otherwise, someone might find your bones in there someday."

Samantha smiled. "Funny."

"Anyway, if you should get stuck, there is an

opening at the top of the elevator. You can crawl through it and you should be able to get in through the door on the floor above."

Samantha looked confused. "You're kidding, aren't you?"

"Nope. Easy to do. Just keep a chair or a ladder in the elevator in case it breaks down."

"Well, that settles that. I won't be using the elevator."

Sven laughed. "Seriously, it's fine to use, but I wouldn't wait too long to have it checked out. Maybe, the fire department does that."

"I'm sure there's a big demand for that here." She thought for a moment. "I would almost bet that this is the only elevator in town," she stated. "I can't remember seeing any buildings in town…"

Sven glanced over at her. "What?"

"Never mind. I forgot about the motel. That has an elevator."

"There you go, Sam. Public elevators must be inspected at least once a year. Ask them who services theirs."

"Good idea."

"Your food will be right up," Cindy told them, as she served them their salads."

"Thanks," Toots said as he picked up his fork. "The salad looks good."

Half an hour later, Samantha sat back and looked at Toot's plate. "It looks like you're finished. Are you ready to leave?"

"Just about. First, let's see what they've got on the menu for dessert."

Chapter Fourteen

"Hi, Mark, it's Samantha."

"How are you two doing out there? Is everything okay?"

"Toots just finished up and everything is locked up tight. Are you at your office?"

"I am. I'll be right over to pick up the keys," Mark replied.

"Don't bother. I'll save you the trip. I've decided that I want the house if we can agree on the price."

"You're going to make an offer?"

"That's the plan."

Mark fist-bumped the air, grinning. Gloria glanced over at him and smiled. "Does she want it?" she mouthed.

Mark shook his head yes. "That's great. I'll get started on the paperwork," he told Samantha.

"I'm just gonna say good-bye to Toots and I'll be right over."

Mark said across the table from Samantha and frowned. "You're not serious?"

"I am totally serious."

"Just the land, without the buildings, is worth more than that."

"The buildings are old and starting to fall apart. I did the research, Mark. That property is priced way too high."

Mark sat back and stared at her. "You're offering $75,000.00 less than the asking price. That's an insult."

"And, the owner is asking $75,000.00 more than it's worth. Besides, how can you refuse my bid when you haven't talked to the seller yet? How do you know he won't go for it?"

"I just know." He stood up. "I'm gonna go get some more coffee. Can I get you anything?"

"I'm good." She watched Mark walk away from the table. Samantha had done her research on the property. She knew every selling price of the house since 1960. Of course, property values had gone up since then, but the house had been empty since Moretti had lived there. The Feds had put it up for auction in 2006 and it had sold for $77,000.00.

Mark walked back into the room and sat down.

"You said that the house is in a trust. Right?" she asked.

"That's correct."

"And, you're the trustee of that trust."

"That's right."

"The people who own it do want to sell it, don't they?"

"They do, but you…"

"Then, why aren't you contacting them? You have a buyer here and you're refusing my offer without even talking to them."

"There is more to it than that."

"I know that house sold for $77,000.00 in 2006. Okay, so that's fourteen years ago, but I don't think it's worth what you're asking."

"That was an auction and that price didn't reflect its real value. But, that's not what I wanted to tell you."

"Oh?"

"To be upfront about it…"

"Yes."

"Well, the truth is…" he hesitated. "I own the house."

Samantha's head jerked up and she stared at Mark. "Are you serious?" she asked, shocked at the news.

Mark looked at her, worried that the deal might go dead. "Sorry," he said. "I guess I should have told you before."

"You think?" Samantha said frowning. "Well, that explains why you know so much about that house. Why didn't you tell me upfront? Now, it looks like you were trying to hide something."

"No, no, Samantha. Not at all. Believe me; I'm not trying to hide anything from you. It isn't required to disclose who the owner is when a property is in a trust."

"So, there's no big dark secret I have to worry about? There are no bodies buried in the basement?"

"None. What you see is what you get."

Samantha shook her head, looking upset. "So, you bought that house for $77,000.00 and are asking three times that? Talk about…"

"Wait," Mark interrupted. "There is more to it than that. My family has owned that property off and on for years but we never lived there. As I mentioned before, Gretchen sold it to some people who tried fox farming. After the fire – I told you about the fire didn't I?"

"You did," Samantha replied.

"Well, after the fire, the place was put up for sale and my grandfather bought it as an investment. He rented it out for years. Then, my dad inherited it and he sold it to Kingsford in 1960. When the Kingsford family put it up for sale, my dad purchased it and, again, rented it out. Eventually, it came to me and I sold it to Carlos Moretti in 2000."

"And, then, you bought it when it was auctioned off six years later," Samantha declared.

"That's right."

"You're doing okay by selling it to me at $160,000.00. That's still a nice profit."

Mark grinned. "Nice try. I haven't agreed to that price. And, it's barely any profit. Not if you start to add up how much that place has cost us over the years. The property taxes have increased every year and we had to fix it up almost every time a renter moved out. At this point, I'm just trying to break even."

"Well, those renters paid rent. It's not like they lived there rent-free. And, from what I see, you certainly didn't lose any money fixing it up." She sat back and smiled. "You didn't even put a fresh coat of paint on that house. You've done okay, Mark, and you know it."

"One seventy-five and it's yours," he said in a soft voice.

Samantha looked at him. "One sixty and that's my final offer."

"You're killing me, Samantha."

"There's a lot of work that needs to be done on that property, Mark. I figure by the time I'm done fixing it up, I'll have close to your original asking price in it." She smiled, waiting for him to respond.

Mark pursed his lips, thinking. He finished off his coffee and put the cup down.

"Well?"

Mark sat back and looked up at the ceiling. "I'm thinking about ..."

"Going – going..." Samantha waited.

"Okay. You have a deal. One-sixty it is."

Samantha grinned. "Gone at $160,000.00. Draw up the papers."

"Congratulations. You got yourself one hell of a deal."

"Thanks. Hey, you wanna go get a drink?"

Mark looked at her and made a face. "I'd rather eat a cockroach."

Samantha laughed. "I feel kinda bad about that. I didn't realize - you know."

"What?"

"That you're a lightweight."

"I'm not a big drinker, but I usually do better than I did last night. Exactly how strong was that whiskey, anyway?"

Samantha smiled. "It's pretty powerful stuff."

"Well, you seem to have handled it a lot better than I did."

"I'm used to it. Plus, I only had two drinks. I wouldn't have been able to get out of bed this morning if I had drunk as much as you did."

Mark sat back in his chair and stared at her. "You could have stopped me."

Samantha grinned. "Hey, you're a big boy and I'm not your mother. Don't blame me if you have a headache."

Mark shook his head, agreeing with her. "You're right. But, damn, it was really smooth going down."

Samantha stood up. "Nothing but the best for my friends," she said smiling.

"Well, then, thanks – I guess. Although, I'd hate to find out what you serve your enemies."

"I don't drink with my enemies, Mark," Samantha

replied. "I'm going back to the motel. I'll stop by in the morning and give you a check for the earnest money and sign the papers."

"Sounds good. How much longer will you be in town?"

"I'm leaving tomorrow right after I see you. I'll be back for the closing. I gather I'll be able to take possession immediately after we close."

"You will."

"What about getting the place cleaned up?"

"I'll get on that right away. There's a lady in town that does one-time cleanings. She's good, but she's also expensive."

"What do you mean expensive?"

"A house that size? It will take her a couple of days – maybe three. Probably around five hundred."

"To clean a house?"

"It will be more than worth it, Samantha. You'll be able to eat off the floors when she's done."

"All right. Give her a call. You're paying for it, so it doesn't make any difference to me how much it costs."

"I'm paying? I don't think so."

"You said you would. Remember?"

"That was before I gave away the house."

Samantha laughed. "Okay, I'll pay for it. By the way, I need a pest control company to fumigate the house. Could you set that up and have that done before the house is cleaned?"

"Fumigated? Why are you having it fumigated?"

"Toots found mice. I would like them gone before I move in. Could you do that for me?"

"I could." Mark sat back and studied her, not saying anything.

"What?" Samantha finally said, starting to feel uncomfortable.

"I hope after you move to town we can be friends. I like you and I'd like to get to know you better."

Samantha felt her cheeks getting warm and knew she was blushing. "Well, that would – I mean..." She smiled. "Thanks, Mark. I think I would like that, too."

"Good." He continued to stare at her.

"I guess I should leave and let you get to work. That contract won't write itself," she said as she stood up.

"Right. I'll take care of the resident mice for you," Mark declared, smiling. "You do realize, don't you, that when you live in the country you have mice?"

Samantha walked towards the door. "It's not the country, it's the edge of town. And, I'll get some cats. What time tomorrow? I'd like to make it early, if possible."

"How's eight?"

"Perfect. I'll see you then."

Mark watched Samantha turn and leave the room. He chuckled to himself as he recalled how he had made her a little uncomfortable.

"Everything okay?"

Mark jumped. He turned to see Gloria standing in the doorway. "Christ, you scared me."

"Soo?"

"She bought it."

"That's great. You want me to write up the contract?"

"Please. There aren't any contingencies and it's a cash deal. She's had it inspected and wants to close as soon as possible."

"Selling price?" Gloria asked.

"$160,000.00," Mark mumbled.

"I'm sorry. I didn't get that."

"$160,000.00," Mark repeated.

Gloria stared at him. "Are you kidding me?"

"I'm still making money. Besides, what do you care?"

"I can't believe you let that place go that cheap, that's all."

Mark looked away. "Can you call Maggie and see if she'll clean that place?"

Gloria didn't say anything.

"One more thing Gloria. We also need to find someone who can fumigate the house before Maggie cleans it. We need to get rid of the mice."

Gloria glared at him.

Mark glanced at her. "Is something wrong? You look upset."

"Is there anything else her royal highness wants?"

"Don't start."

"You've got the hots for her, don't you?"

"What the hell are you talking about, Gloria?"

"Why else would you agree to that selling price?"

"That's enough. It's none of your business what I sold that house for."

Gloria studied him, trying to figure out if he was lying to her. "She's pretty good-looking, isn't she?"

Mark shook his head and sighed. "Enough. You do this every time a woman comes through the door. I'm tired of your crap."

"You didn't answer me, Mark. Do you have the hots for her? What went on with you two last night?"

"I'm not having this conversation again, so just

drop it."

"I swear, Mark, if I find out that you slept with that bitch, I'll fucking kill her."

Chapter Fifteen

She was tired and crabby, so when Mark called her for the third time that day she wasn't in the mood to have another conversation with him.

"What now?" she sighed as she answered his call.

"I just thought I'd check in with you before I leave the office," he told her. "Are you okay? Do you need anything?"

"I need to be left alone!" Samantha barked.

"Whoa! I'm sorry I called," Mark replied, taken back by her outburst. "I guess I caught you at a bad time."

Samantha took a deep breath and let it out. "I'm sorry I snapped, Mark. I'm just really tired and I'm not in the mood for conversation."

"I'll let you go, then," Mark said. "I'm sorry I bothered you. Good night, Samantha."

"Wait," she called out. "Don't hang up."

"What?"

"I really am sorry. What are you doing Saturday night?"

"I'm free. Why?"

"Would you like to come over for dinner? I have a couple of steaks that need to be thawed out. Are you interested?"

Mark sat back in his desk chair and smiled. He put his feet up on his desk and took a long swallow of his beer. "I do the grilling – right?"

"After what happened last time, I think you're the only one qualified to do the grilling. I know when to step back and let an expert do it."

"It sounds good. What time would you like me there?"

"Let's say six-thirty."

"I'll be there. Can I bring anything?"

"Nope. I think I'm good." She hesitated a second. "Unless..."

"What?"

"You could bring a bottle of wine if you want. I'll probably finish off whatever wine I have in the house before Saturday."

"Wine it is. Red or white?"

"I don't care. Bring whatever you want."

"I'll bring one of each. How's that?"

"Great. I'll see you Saturday."

"I'm looking forward..." he shook his head, realizing that she had already ended the call.

"Mark?"

Mark practically jumped out of his chair. He turned and saw Gloria standing in the doorway."

"Fuck, Gloria," he yelled. "You scared the shit out of me. You have to stop sneaking up behind me. Do I have to start locking the fucking door to keep you from eavesdropping?"

"I wasn't eavesdropping, so stop the dramatics. I just wanted to let you know that you have a client waiting."

Mark looked confused. "I don't recall making an appointment with anyone."

"You didn't. It's a walk-in. Do you want me to tell him to leave?"

"Of course not. Show him in."

"Will do," Gloria said. As she turned to leave the

room, she looked back at Mark. "You might want to get rid of the beer."

Mark finished off what was left in the bottle and tossed it in the wastebasket. "Okay, it's gone," he said, grinning.

"It's red, you know."

"What's red?" he asked, looking confused.

"The wine. You should serve red wine with red meat," Gloria told him. "I thought you knew that."

Samantha turned off the shower and grabbed a towel. She wrapped it around her body and stepped onto the plush bathmat.

She smiled as she thought about Mark coming over on Saturday. Since she had moved to Columbus, she had kept to herself except for the occasional meal with him. *It will be nice to have some company*, she thought.

She threw on a terry cloth robe, slipped into a pair of slippers, and walked down a flight of stairs to the kitchen.

After Samantha took possession of the house, she decided to start her search outside. The weather would be warm for another few months, and she would work inside the house when it cooled down.

The tool shed was the first building to go. After it was demolished, she used her metal detector to determine if anything had been buried in the ground beneath it. She got a few solid beeps, but after digging up a few nails she decided to try a new location.

Samantha knew that in the early 2000s, after Moretti had been arrested, the feds had done a complete GPR search of the property. However, as far as she could determine, no metal detecting had been done at that time.

She researched metal detectors and finally settled on one manufactured by Garrett's. It was powerful but it was also heavy, weighing around eight pounds. Samantha could only use it for an hour or so before her arm got tired and she needed to rest. So far, nothing had yielded any results.

When the weather was rainy, she searched inside the house. The attic was the first place she looked. It was small and she had a little difficulty in checking it out on her stomach. However, it was obvious that there were no hiding places up there, and she scratched that off her list of places to search.

Working down from the attic, Samantha searched the fourth and third floors of the house. She had been surprised at how easy it had been to break through the plaster walls. It had made one hell of a mess. However, seeing as how she had no intention of making any repairs, she had no intention of cleaning it up.

The garage would be the last place she would check. Colder weather was coming and she wanted to be able to use the garage as long as possible.

Samantha opened the refrigerator and took out a half-empty bottle of wine. She poured most of it into a wine glass, took a long drink, and emptied what was left in the bottle into her glass.

She picked up the glass, walked into the living room, and sat down.

"God, I'm tired," she mumbled. She took another sip of wine, set the glass on an end table, and reached for the TV remote.

She was startled when her phone rang, disturbing

the silence of the room. She laughed as she answered her cell phone. "Toots. I was just thinking about you. Are we still on for tomorrow?"

"We are. I reserved a backhoe from the John Deere place in Columbus. I think we'll go straight there, pick it up, and then come to you."

"Are you in Rockford?"

"Yeah. Joyce came with me, so she'll stay and visit while Gary and I drive up."

"Gary's coming? That's great. I haven't seen him since I can't remember when. It will be good to see him?"

"I'll see you tomorrow, Sam."

"Thank you for this, Toots. I owe you big. You know, I never would have bothered you if I could have done this myself. I mean, that metal detector went nuts. I can't ignore it."

"Stop it. You know that there is nothing in this world that I wouldn't do for you. Anyway, this sounds interesting."

"This could be it, you know."

"Let's hope."

Chapter Sixteen

Samantha moved the metal detector back and forth over the pile of dirt. Gary gave her a questioning look and she shook her head no. "Not yet," she yelled. She stepped back as Toots scooped up more dirt and dropped it.

"Something's in there!" Gary shouted, pointing to an object sticking up out of the dirt. He walked a little closer to the pile, reached over, and pulled out a long white object. He looked at it for a moment and suddenly dropped it. He motioned to Toots to cut the engine on the backhoe.

"What is it?" Samantha asked him.

"It looks like a bone. A human bone," Gary told her.

"Why would it be buried here?" Samantha asked.

Toots got off the backhoe and walked over to the pile of dirt. He picked up the bone and studied it. "You may be right, Gary. I think it is a leg bone and it looks like it's been buried for a long time."

"Why would a leg bone be buried here?" Samantha asked again.

Toots turned and glanced at the barn. "This is where the pigsty was, isn't it?"

"That's what I was told. This is where the pigs rolled around in the mud all day."

"Whattaya thinking, Toots?" Gary asked.

"I'm gonna dig a little deeper. Something set off that detector. We need to find out what it is."

"Well, we know it wasn't that bone. Bones

90

wouldn't set off the detector," Samantha said.

Toots climbed back onto the backhoe, scooped up another load of dirt, and dropped it.

Gary swept the pile with the detector, grinning as it sent out a high-pitched beep. "We got something," he yelled as he grabbed his hand trowel and started probing the dirt.

"What is it?" Samantha asked excitedly.

Gary held up a large metal belt buckle. "It looks like this is your culprit," he said as he handed it to her.

"A belt buckle? A stinking belt buckle?" Samantha muttered. "Are you kidding me?"

"It looks really old. It could be worth something," Gary stated.

"Gary, check down there," Toots yelled as he pointed at the dirt. "There's something else there."

Gary looked at where Toots was pointing and swore. "Shit! It looks like another bone, Toots." He walked over to where Toots had pointed and carefully brushed away some dirt. He looked up at Toots. "It's a skull. It looks like a body was buried here. Do you think we need to get the police out here?"

"No!" Samantha shouted. "I don't want the cops out here."

"We don't have a choice, Sam," Toots told her. "This could be a crime scene. Obviously, someone is buried here."

"I don't care. Just throw those bones back in the hole and cover them up. You said that bone was old and it was the buckle that set off the detector, so let's just put everything back the way it was."

Gary shook his head. "No. It's not that simple, Samantha. We need to do the right thing."

"What are you gonna tell them when they ask why we were digging a hole where there used to be a pigsty?"

"I don't know. We'll think of something," Toots replied. "

"I think we should cover it up and forget about it."

"Hold on a minute. Let me go over that area again," Gary said as he jumped down into the shallow hole that Toots had dug. He swept the metal detector across the area and grinned when the detector let out a series of shrill beeps. "There's something else down there, Toots. It can't be too far down. How about we dig a little more before we call the cops?"

"I'm afraid I'm gonna smash that skull."

Gary bent down and gently removed the dirt from around the skull, picked it up, and held it out for Samantha to take it.

"I'm not touching that," she exclaimed.

"Come on, don't be a baby. Take it. It's not gonna bite you," he said teasingly.

"No."

Laughing, Gary stepped up out of the hole. "You're just a little fraidy cat," he said, as he pretended to throw the skull at her.

"Stop it, Gary. I mean it," Samantha said. "That's somebody's head you're messing with."

Gary laughed and put the skull down next to the leg bone.

Toots dumped another bucket of dirt and watched Gary check it with the metal detector. He smiled when the detector went off again. "Another hit," he yelled

Gary pinpointed the ping, reached down, and picked something up. "It's a ring. It looks like a man's wedding band."

"Let me see," Samantha said holding out her hand. She took the ring from Gary and looked at it. "I'll be right back," she said as she walked towards the house.

"Where are you going?" Gary asked.

"I want to wash this off," she yelled over her shoulder. "Keep digging."

"Check it again, Gary," Toots said. "Let's see if we get any more hits."

Samantha, Toots, and Gary stared at the middle of the kitchen table.

"We found a belt buckle, a man's wedding ring, a woman's diamond ring, and a couple of gold teeth. I wonder what that will bring us split three ways?" Samantha asked.

"It sure as hell isn't going to make us rich," Gary told her.

"Don't forget about the bones," Toots added.

"I'd like to," Samantha told him. "I'd like to forget about those two teeth, too. They freak me out."

"Who do you suppose the rings belonged to?" Toots asked.

"I guess they could have belonged to anyone," Samantha commented.

"I figure the teeth and the man's ring belong to whoever Mr. Bones is," Gary said. He looked over at Samantha. "What areas do you have left to search?"

"The barn, the garage, the rest of the..." She got up from the table and looked out of the window. "I've barely scratched the surface. I'm so stupid to think I can do this all by myself. It's just too much for one person."

"Are you sure it's here?" Toots asked.

Samantha shrugged. "I'm pretty sure. Although, there's the possibility that someone who lived here found it after Moretti was arrested. This place was rented out a lot after that happened. But, I think we would have heard about it if someone had found a bunch of money."

"Let's go over this again," Toots suggested. "Let's see if I have it right."

"Alright," Samantha said. "Let's start with Frank Costa who was Gino Costa's nephew."

Gary looked confused. "I'm not familiar with the Costas. Who are they?"

"Gino Costa was one of Carlos Moretti's soldiers," Samantha told Gary. "Frank Costa and his wife were hired to take care of this place when Moretti owned it. It was a safe haven for Moretti's men when they needed to lay low for a while. Sometimes, crime lords from all over the country would meet here."

"This doesn't ring a bell at all. I can't remember hearing about this Moretti guy."

"It was big news in 2005. I think you were living in France during that time," Toots told him.

"You're right. I was. So, this place has history," Gary commented.

"That's not all," Toots told him. "It was also used as a dumping ground for bodies."

"Well, that accounts for the bones we found," Gary stated.

"I don't think so, Gary. The six bodies that were found were buried in the field behind the house. It was determined that they had died between 2001 and 2005. The bones we found today are a lot older than that. I think whoever we found today died a long time ago," Samantha told him.

"Go on with your story. What happened to Kari and Frank Costa?" Gary asked.

"A few weeks after Carlos Moretti and his gang were arrested, the Feds arrested Kari and Frank. That happened in 2005. They were tried, convicted, and sent to prison. Frank was murdered in prison a few years before his sentence was up," Toots told him. "Kari served seven years of a ten-year sentence. She died shortly after she was released from prison."

"How old was she when she died?" Gary asked.

Samantha thought for a moment. "She wasn't that old. I think she was like, maybe forty-five or so. She had terminal cancer, which is one of the reasons she was let out of prison early."

"And, Sam's mother was her nurse," Toots added.

"Well, not so much her nurse as her caregiver," Samantha corrected. "Mom was in her seventies but she was active and pretty sharp. She would occasionally volunteer her services when a terminally ill person couldn't afford to hire someone. She would check in on Kari, read to her, do her shopping, and... You know, just help her with the basics," Samantha said.

"Why do you think Kari told your mom about the money? Why not tell one of her relatives or..."

"Kari didn't have any children or siblings," Samantha said, interrupting Gary. "Her parents died when she was young and, as far as she knew, she didn't have any other relatives. My mom spent a lot of time with her while she was ill. Kari told her stories about her life, including the time that she and her husband worked for Moretti. I guess it just came up during one of the conversations."

"And, she knows for a fact that Moretti hid money here?" Gary asked.

"My mom seemed convinced that it was true. Kari tended to repeat things but the story never changed. Well, except for the endings. Sometimes, Kari would add something that she hadn't mentioned before. Anyway, my mom figured Kari knew what she was talking about. Before my mom died, she told me about it and suggested I check it out." She picked up her coffee cup and took a sip of coffee. "It seems that Moretti figured if he had to get out of the country in a hurry, he would have a stash here to take with him. It's supposed to still be here." Samantha shrugged. "I don't know, Toots. Maybe it is all made up. But, if the story is true, there could be a frickin' fortune here – someplace."

"There are a million hiding places here, Sam. I told you that before you bought this place. You could spend the next two or three years searching and never find anything. I think you need help."

"I agree, Sam," Gary said. "You can't do this by yourself."

"Well, what do you suggest I do?" she asked.

Toots looked at Gary. "How about it?" he asked.

"Me?" Gary said, laughing nervously. "No way."

"Why not? You're not doing much these days except playing golf and getting fat. Why not help Sam out?"

"You seriously think I want to live here?" Gary asked.

"It wouldn't be forever. Just until you find the money." Toots looked at Samantha. "What do you say, Sam? Do you want some company?"

Samantha pursed her lips, thinking. "I don't know. I guess I could use some muscle and Gary certainly has an abundance of those. Maybe some help isn't a bad idea. What would you want if you did help out, Gary?"

Gary shrugged. "I don't know. I guess it would depend on what we find." He looked at her. "Do you have any idea of what kind of money we're talking about?"

Samantha glanced over at Toots.

"Tell him," he told her.

"If – and that's a big if – the story is true..." She hesitated.

"Tell him, Sam," Toots said.

"There could be close to eight to ten million dollars buried here somewhere."

Gary's jaw dropped. "No shit!" He stared at her. "How would you even know that, Sam?"

"That's what my mom told me."

Chapter Seventeen

(2001)

"What do you think you're doing?"

Kari looked at her husband and grinned. "Look at this, Frankie. There must be hundreds of thousands of dollars here."

Frank stared at the pile of money and felt his stomach turn over. "For God's sake, put it back, Kari. If Carlos knew you were snooping around in here, he'd kill you."

"Well, he's not here, is he? So, how could he find out unless you tell him? Besides, he knows I come in here."

"To clean – yes. But, not to snoop in his drawers. Put it back, Kari."

"Do you think he'd miss a couple hundred dollars?"

"I think he'd know if fifty cents was missing. Don't even think about it, Kari. You'll get us both killed."

She picked up a handful of money and smelled it. "We could disappear, Frank. We could get out of this stink hole and go live on a tropical beach somewhere. How does that sound?"

"You know I burn easily," he said joking.

"Which is why they make sunscreen." She smiled up at Frank. "Every time he comes here, the pile gets bigger, you know."

Frank stared at her. "How long have you known about this money?"

"Ever since he started stashing it away. I figure he's dropping forty to fifty grand in the pile every time he comes up

here. Sometimes, more."

Frank stared at her. "Please tell me that you've never taken any of it."

Kari grinned. "Don't worry. I don't have a death wish. I just enjoy looking at it every so often, that's all."

Frank stared at the money. "You need to put it back and we need to get out of here."

"All right. Geez, I'm not hurting anything, you know."

Frank watched as Kari carefully put the money back into the bottom drawer of a dresser. She made sure everything was neat and closed the drawer. "Happy now?"

"No. And, I won't be as long as that money's in the house. Just promise me that you'll stay out of that drawer from now on."

"Ah, Frankie, do I have to promise? You know I have so little to look forward to." She stood on her tiptoes and kissed him.

Frank put his hands on her shoulders and looked her in the eyes. "Promise me, Kari."

"Really?"

"Kari. I mean it."

"I promise."

"The thing is," Samantha said, "Kari didn't keep that promise. She continued to check that drawer whenever she got the chance. And, then, one day – boom! The money was gone."

"So, who took it?" Gary asked.

"Oh, no. No one took it, but it had been moved."

"By who?"

"Moretti, of course."

"Did she ever find the new location?"

Samantha let out a sigh. "She did, but..."

(2003)

"Carlos called," Frank told Kari. "He wants us to go away for a few days. He's already made a reservation for us at the Dells and he's paying for it."

"Why?" Kari asked, looking surprised.

"He said that everyone deserves a vacation now and then. We're supposed to leave Friday and come back Monday morning."

"Well, that's a bunch of bullshit. Do you know the real reason he wants us out of here for the weekend?"

"Nope. All I know is what he told me."

Kari shrugged. "Well, I was never one to look a gift horse in the mouth. It might be fun to spend a few days playing in the water."

"He told me to leave the key under the mat by the back door."

"For who?"

"I have no idea. Just make sure I don't forget."

I'd give anything to know what's going on here this weekend," Kari said. "Do you think it's another body dump?"

"I doubt it. He didn't ask me to dig any holes."

"According to what Kari told my mom, she and

Frank drove back from the Dells on Sunday night instead of Monday. They noticed a lot of cars parked by the house, so they drove on by. They decided to kill some time and go get something to eat. When they drove back to the house a few hours later, all the cars were gone and the house was dark. The house looked the same on the inside as it had when they left except for one thing."

"What was that?" Gary asked, totally engrossed in the story Samantha was telling.

"Kari noticed sawdust on the floor."

"Sawdust?"

"Yup. Sawdust. Well, Kari, being about as nosy as a person could be, decided to check out the house to see if she could find where it had come from."

"Sam, I'm growing old here," Toots told her, smiling. "Get to the point, will you?"

"Sorry. I'm just about finished. Anyhow, she checked out the dresser drawer and found it was empty. Her first thought was that Moretti had taken the money with him, but she found sawdust in several more places. No matter how long and hard she looked, she couldn't find anything that would have caused the sawdust."

"Come on, Sam," Toots urged. "Get to the end, will ya?"

"Stop rushing her, Toots," Gary said.

Samantha smiled. "Thank you, Gary. Anyway, to make a long story even longer, she eventually found the new hiding place. She continued to check its contents every so often. She's the one who estimated the amount of money that Moretti had here." Samantha glanced at the diamond ring, picked it up, and studied it for a moment. "This looks familiar," she murmured as she placed it back on the table. "I would swear I've seen this ring before."

(1941)

"Gretchen, are you feeling okay?" John asked his daughter as she walked up to him. "You don't look well."

"Where's Ray?"

"What do you mean, girl? You know that Ray is dead."

"Where did you put him, Father? I need to see his grave."

"No, you don't. He's gone and that's all you need to know. You need to forget about him and what happened. We all need to put it behind us."

"I'm carrying his child. How can I put what happened behind me? What will I tell my children when they ask about their father?"

"You lie," John told her. "He disappeared one night. That's all you know. That's all you tell them."

"It haunts me, you know. I dream about him lying there with that big hole in his chest. It's horrible." Gretchen looked at her father, her eyes pleading with him to help her. "I need closure. Where did you put him?"

"Where no one will ever find him, Gretchen. You don't have to worry."

"I'll ask mother. She'll tell me where he is," Gretchen said and turned back towards the house.

"Wait."

Gretchen turned and looked at her father. "What?"

"You won't like it."

"Please, tell me."

John reached out and took her hand. "This way," he said softly and led her towards the barn. "He's there," he said pointing at the pigsty.

Gretchen's face turned white as the news sunk in. She looked up at her father. "You fed him to the pigs?" she whispered.

"I did."

She stared at the pigs that were rooting around in the mud. "He's really gone, isn't he?"

"You don't need to worry about him, Gretchen. He can't hurt you anymore."

Gretchen pulled her wedding rings off of her finger and threw them into the pigsty. "It's fitting," she told her father. "He was a pig. He should rot here for eternity," she said, crying softly.

John pulled his daughter close to him and held her. "It's time to move on," he told her.

"Forget about the ring. Where's the money?" Gary asked.

Samantha stared at him. "Well, stupid, if I knew where it was, don't you think I'd have it by now?"

Toots laughed. "Finish your story."

Samantha smiled. "That's where the story gets confusing. The money should be in the house, but I can't find it. Kari told this story to my mother several times, but she would never say exactly where the hiding place is. She would say things like 'I finally looked up and found it' or 'I looked down and there it was.' She would never say exactly where. Sometimes I think she was just playing mind games with my mom, but my mother thought she was telling the truth. So, I thought maybe..."

"A well, Sam," Toots interrupted. "Maybe, it's down a well."

"I already thought of that. There was a well here years ago but it was filled in long before Moretti lived here. Anyway, I thought that Moretti must have buried it. But, I just can't..." Samantha looked away, shaking her head in frustration.

"You know a metal detector isn't going to pick up a bag of money that's been buried," Toots stated.

Samantha sighed. "I know that but you never know what a person is thinking when they do stuff."

"No, you're wrong. It's not out there. I think you're way off base looking outside," Gary said getting excited.

"What do you mean?" Samantha asked him.

"I think the money is in the house. It has to be. Moretti would never risk burying it outside. He would put it where it would be easy to get at, yet hard to find. You've only searched the attic and two floors. We've got to absolutely tear this place apart. We'll gut it if we have to."

"I guess that makes sense," Samantha said.

"Sam, are you sure your mother got the amount right?" Gary asked.

Samantha shook her head yes. "Mom spent a lot of time with Kari. She told me that each time Kari repeated this story, she added a little more information. Mom figures that Kari was eventually going to tell her where the hiding place was, but she took a turn for the worse and within a few days, she was gone. I think the story is true, Gary. One hundred percent true."

He smiled at Samantha. "Well, I'll tell you this, sweetheart. If that money is here, we're gonna find it. You and I are gonna tear this place apart."

Toots grinned. "I take it you're in," he said, looking at Gary.

"Hell, yes, I'm in. Let's find that money."

Toots grinned. "Okay, then, let's decide on the split."

Samantha stared at him. "What do you mean, the split?"

"You don't expect Gary to help you for nothing, do you?"

"He doesn't need the money."

"Come on, Sam. Be nice," Toots told her.

Sam thought about it for a moment. "How much are you talking about?"

"What are you willing to part with, Sam, if you find it?"

"One-fourth," she answered without giving it a second thought.

Gary smiled. "I don't think so."

"That's a fair offer, Gary," Samantha said.

"One-third," Gary said, grinning.

Samantha glanced over at Toots. "What do you think?"

Toots smiled. "That sounds fair to me. The rest is yours."

"What about you, Toots?" she asked, surprised. You should get a share."

"Nah. What do I need it for? I've already got more money than Joyce can spend. And, believe me, she spends a lot. You can take us to dinner some time. How's that?"

"That's not right. You should get something for your time and trouble," Samantha told him.

"I need a new truck. How about you buy me a new truck? But, only if you find your hidden treasure. How's that?"

Samantha grinned. "Deal," she said.

"Okay, splitting up money we don't have and may never have is settled," Gary said. "What next?"

"Let's go put those bones back," Toots said. He reached over and picked up the gold teeth that were on the table. "These go, too," he said as he placed them next to the bones.

"Can we get that stuff off the table?" Samantha asked. "It makes me uncomfortable."

Toots sat back and smiled. "Gary, would you like to take care of that? Right now I could go for a cold one. Do you have any beer, Sam?"

Samantha took a couple of bottles of beer out of the refrigerator and set them on the table."

"Do you have an opener?" Toots asked.

"Here you go," she said as she handed him a bottle opener. "So, when are you going back to Rockford?" she asked.

"As soon as we're done outside." Toots was quiet for a few moments. "Gary, you should probably drive back with me so you can pick up some extra clothes and stuff."

"That's a good idea." He smiled at Samantha.

"What are you smiling about?" she asked him.

"We're gonna be roomies."

Toots laughed. "It's a shame I can't be a fly on the wall for the next few weeks."

"You do realize you will be sleeping in your own

106

room in your own bed, don't you?" Samantha asked, frowning.

"Come on, Samantha. Don't be like that." Gary said. He took a sip of his beer and grinned.

"I sleep with a loaded gun under my pillow, Gary," Samantha told him with a straight face.

"I hear ya. Anyway, no worries. You'll give in soon enough. All I have to do is wait for you to get a little horny and you'll be all over me."

"In your dreams, mister. Only in your dreams."

"This might not be such a good idea after all," Toots said after listening to the two of them go at it.

"We're fine, Toots." She looked at Gary. "You get Saturdays and Sundays off, you know."

"I do?" Gary inquired. "Why is that?"

"Well, you get this weekend off anyway. I have plans. Don't come back until Monday."

Toots looked up, surprised. "I thought you stayed away from these town people."

"It's just a friend coming for dinner. No big deal, Toots."

Toots studied her face for a moment. "He's good?"

"Not to worry. He knows nothing and nothing is going on between us. It's Mark. You've met him."

"Right. I'm just a little surprised that you're friends with him. You've never said anything about him."

"It's nice to have a little company once in a while. He's the only person I know here in town. Most of the people around here think I'm the crazy lady who bought the Box House. For the most part, they stay away from me."

"What about the backhoe? Should we return it

after we rebury that stuff?" Gary asked Toots, changing the subject.

"I rented it for the month. You may have a use for it. Why don't you park it in the barn for now?"

"Okay, then. Everything is settled. How about I make us some lunch while you finish up outside?" Samantha asked. "I don't know about you guys, but I'm starving."

Chapter Eighteen

Mark grabbed his beer and took a big swallow. He looked up and smiled as Samantha came out of the back door of the house. "The steaks are just about ready," he called out.

"Are the potatoes done?"

"They're perfect," Mark said.

"Good. I made a salad and the table is set." She smiled at him. "This is nice. I'm glad you came over."

"I wouldn't miss a free meal for anything," he said, smiling back at her. "Or, your company," he added.

"Well, somehow, it doesn't seem right that I ask you over and then you do all the work."

"I enjoy grilling..." He turned and looked towards the front of the house as a car pulled in and stopped. "It looks like you've got company," he declared.

Samantha frowned when she saw who was in the car. "Damn him," she swore under her breath.

"Who is it?" Mark asked, standing up.

Gary got out of the car, grinning. "Looks like I'm just in time for dinner," he said as he walked towards Samantha.

"What the hell, Gary? What are you doing here?"

"I figured I'd get a head start and come up today instead of Monday." He glanced over at Mark.

"Mark, this is Gary, my cousin," Samantha said.

Gary masked his surprise and grinned. "It's nice to meet you, Mark. So, you're the person that sold my little Sam this monstrosity," Gary said, as he reached out to shake Mark's hand.

"I'm sorry, Mark. Gary thinks he's funny." She turned and glared at Gary. "And, he's not funny at all. Are you, Gary?"

Gary shrugged. "Hey, I try."

"Well, maybe you should try harder," she snapped at him.

Gary looked surprised at her outburst. "Sorry, I guess I caught you at a bad time, Sam. So, if you'll excuse me, I'll get out of your hair and let you guys enjoy your meal." He glanced over at the grill. "I think those are done," he told Mark. "I'll just get my suitcase and go make myself comfortable in my room. You won't even know I'm here."

Samantha watched as Gary walked back to his car and got a suitcase out of the trunk. He smiled as he walked by them. "Man, those steaks sure smell good," he remarked as he went into the house.

"I'm gonna kill him," Samantha muttered under her breath.

"Plates," Mark called out as he checked the steaks.

"What?"

"Plates. The steaks are ready."

"Sorry," Samantha said, as she ran into the house.

"It's getting late. I guess I should go," Mark said as he looked at his watch.

"It's only a little after nine," Samantha said, glancing at the clock on the wall. "It's still early."

Mark finished off his glass of wine and looked around the room. "It doesn't look like you've done much decorating since the last time I was here. The place looks the same."

"I still have a lot of things at my home in Chicago. I'll clear it out after it sells. I've been told that when you're trying to sell a house, it presents better when it's furnished."

"It usually does," Mark agreed.

"The wine was good," Samantha commented.

"Yes, it was. It looks like you've been doing some digging outside."

"A little," she replied.

"Looking for anything special?"

"Not really."

Mark picked up his wine glass and looked at it.

"I'd offer you more wine, but unfortunately, we ran out," Samantha said.

"No. I'm good. Believe me, I've had enough," Mark told her.

"If I'd known there would be a third person here tonight, I would have had another bottle on hand," she said, through clenched teeth, as she shot daggers at Gary.

"Hey," Gary exclaimed, holding up his hands. "You invited me to eat with you. I didn't ask."

"Well, you could hardly expect us to enjoy our meal knowing you were in your room pouting. Thanks for that, Gary."

"I wasn't pouting. I don't pout," Gary said, as he stuck out his lower lip.

Mark wiped his mouth with his napkin and stood up. "I think I'll leave, Samantha. Thank you for dinner." He turned and looked at Gary. "Nice meeting you, Gary. It certainly has been an interesting evening."

"Really, Mark, you don't have..."

"I think it's best if I do," Mark interrupted. "Obviously, you need to have some alone time with your cousin and sort out some things." He bent down and kissed Samantha on the cheek. "I'll talk to you later."

"Thanks, Mark."

"He seems like a nice guy," Gary said, as Mark closed the door.

Samantha turned, looked at Gary, and screamed, "What the hell is wrong with you? I told you I had plans for this weekend!"

"I missed you, Sam."

She stared at him and yelled. "You're dead meat. I'm gonna fuckin' kill you, Gary."

"I have something for you," he told her, smiling.

Samantha rolled her eyes. "God, give me strength."

"I'll be right back." Gary got up and walked out of the house.

Samantha stood and stared at the door. "What the hell?" She waited a moment wondering if asking Gary to help her was a big mistake.

Gary walked back into the house, grinning. "I didn't come empty-handed, Sam."

Samantha stared at Gary, who was carrying a case of wine, and shook her head in disbelief. "Are you kidding me?"

Gary grinned. "We are gonna have so much fun, Samantha."

"This isn't going to work." She grabbed her phone. "I need to call Toots."

Chapter Nineteen

Samantha handed the phone to Gary. "Toots wants to talk to you."

"What's up, Toots?" Gary asked as he put the phone to his ear. "Right. I know." He glanced over at Samantha. "Yeah, but..." He listened to Toots. "I will. I'll tell her right now." He shook his head. "No, I understand." He handed the phone back to Samantha.

"Is everything okay, Toots?" She smiled. "Thank you. Love you, too." She ended the call and stared at Gary.

"Okay. I'm sorry," he said. "I was totally out of line and I should have waited until tomorrow night to come back here."

"That's right. You should have. What I'm doing here isn't fun and games. This is serious shit, Gary. I've got a lot of money invested in this house – this..." She took a deep breath and let it out.

"I really am sorry, Sam. I acted like an ass. Can we forget about it and start over? I'll even call Mark and apologize if that will help."

Samantha stared at him for a moment. "Oh, to hell with it. I'll talk to Mark tomorrow. Right now, I'm tired and I'm going to bed."

Gary glanced over to the corner of the room. "Does that thing work?" he asked, pointing at the elevator.

"I guess. At least it did when Toots checked out the house. I haven't used it, though. Toots said not to use it until I got somebody to check it out. Seeing as how I'm only using the first two floors, I didn't see the need to call anyone."

"Well, I could take a look at it for you," Gary volunteered.

"How much do you know about elevators?"

Gary grinned. "Nothing."

"That's what I figured. Good night, Gary."

"My room is right next to yours," Gary stated.

Samantha turned and stared at him. "So?"

"I just hope you don't snore, that's all. Good night, Sam."

Samantha opened her eyes, sat up, and turned on the light next to her bed. "That's it!" she exclaimed. She jumped out of bed, yelling for Gary as she threw on a robe.

"Gary," she yelled for the second time, as she hurried to his room. "Are you awake," she shouted, as she pounded on his door.

"I am now," Gary said sleepily. "What's going on?"

"Get out here. Hurry," she cried out.

Gary swung open the door. "What's the matter? Are you okay?"

Samantha stared at him for a second. "I think I..." She looked away. "Would you mind putting some pants on?"

Gary looked down and grinned. "Sorry. I'll just be a sec."

Samantha waited while he pulled on a pair of jeans.

"Is that better?"

"You have no idea. Thank you."

"So, do you wanna tell me what the ruckus is all about, or do you always run around yelling at three in the morning?"

"I think I know where the money is hidden."

Gary grinned. "No way! Where? Where is it?"

Suddenly Samantha stopped smiling and frowned. "Wait a minute. If I'm right and we do find the money, you don't still expect me to give you one-third, do you? After all, you haven't done anything to help. In fact, since you got here, all you've done is piss me off."

Gary glared at her. "A deal is a deal, Sam."

"But, you haven't done anything."

"You have to be fucking kidding me. Are you actually going to go back on your word?"

Samantha shrugged. "You haven't done anything," she repeated softly.

"And, what do you think Toots would say about this? Huh?"

"I think he would say I'm right."

"No, he wouldn't and you know it."

"Well, then I think we should call Toots and ask him. We'll let him have the final word. Whattaya say?"

Gary didn't say anything, trying to control his anger.

"Well?"

"He'll side with you. He likes you better than me."

Samantha laughed. "What are you? Five?"

"You agreed, Sam."

"How about I give you maybe ten or fifteen percent of what we find? That's not bad for not doing anything."

"You don't even know if it's there for sure," Gary said. "Twenty-five percent. I'll settle for twenty-five if we find it tonight."

Samantha shook her head no. "I don't think so. I'm going back to bed. I'll call Toots first thing in the morning and see what he has to say."

Gary took a step towards her. "Sleep with me – right now - and you don't have to give me anything."

"Do you seriously think that one night with me is worth that much?" Samantha asked grinning.

Gary shrugged. "I have no idea, but I'd sure as hell like to find out."

Samantha laughed. "Well, seeing as how Toots seems to be our referee about everything lately, maybe we should ask him if I should do that, too."

"Forget it," Gary said, as he turned and walked back into his bedroom. "I think we better leave Toots out of it."

Samantha ended the call and laid her cell on the table. "Well, that's that, then. Twenty percent, it is."

"Right. Unless it's not there. Then, we are back to our original agreement of one-third."

"Do you want some more coffee?" she asked.

"Nope, I'm gonna finish dressing. Where are your tools?"

"Most of them are up on the third floor. How are we going to do this?"

"Do you have a step ladder?"

"There's one in the garage."

"All right, I'll get that. I'll need a hammer and a crowbar."

"Third floor. I'll get those," Samantha said.

"Do you have a power drill?"

"You mean like for drilling holes?"

Gary smiled. "Yes."

"It's around here someplace. It might be in the basement."

"Could you take a look? I might need it."

"Where are you going to start?" Samantha asked.

"I'll check the top first. If it's not there, we'll have to bring the elevator up so I can get at the bottom. He smiled at her. "I can't believe it came to you while you were sleeping."

"I know. Weird, isn't it? I was dreaming about my mother and she was singing this nonsense song." She thought for a moment. "We all look up – we all look down," she sang. "Then, sawdust was floating in the air and the sawdust turned into money and the money was floating - well, you know how messed up dreams are."

Gary finished off his coffee and put the dirty cup in the sink. "That's really weird. I'll go get dressed, then," he said not moving.

Samantha waited. "Did you mean today?"

He grinned. "I've got butterflies in my stomach. I can't believe how nervous I am."

"It may not be there, you know."

"I know. But, how sweet would it be if it is?" Gary muttered as he walked out of the kitchen.

Chapter Twenty

"I lost count," Samantha said, giggling.

"Then you must start over," Gary told her.

"I don't think I can count that high."

Gary carefully wrapped a rubber band around a stack of bills and placed them in a suitcase. "Can you keep it together, Sam? We're almost done here."

Samantha reached for a glass of wine. "This is some pretty good shit you brought me up here."

Gary shook his head. "You need to go sleep it off. I'll finish up."

"We should call Tootsie baby and tell him we found the money."

"We already did. He's on his way up here and I don't think he'll be very happy to see the condition you're in."

Samantha stared at him. "Toots is coming here?"

"For God's sake, Sam, get your shit together, will you?"

"I need coffee."

"You need a nap."

"No way, José! I'm not leaving you alone with my money."

Gary shook his head. "God, you're a pain in the ass." He got up off the floor and walked towards the kitchen. "I'll go put on a pot of coffee."

Samantha smiled sweetly. "Thank you, Gary," she said softly as she sprawled out on the carpet and fell asleep.

"Damn, that's a lot of money!" Toots exclaimed. "I can't believe you found it." He looked across the table at Samantha. "You look like crap."

She grinned. "But, I feel like a million dollars. No. Wait. I feel like seven million dollars."

Gary filled Samantha's coffee cup and handed it to her. "Drink," he ordered.

"I've had enough. Anymore of your coffee and I'll be awake for a month." She pushed the cup away. "What do I do now, Toots?"

"What do you mean, Sam?"

"Well, I can't walk around with all that money and I sure can't just go stick it in some bank."

"I have some connections that can help you with this. You'll have to open up an account in..." He looked at Gary. "The Cayman Islands or Switzerland? What do you think, Gary?"

"I use a Swiss bank myself. I prefer it to the Cayman Islands. But, I love to ski, so I go visit my money from time to time and get in a little skiing while I'm there."

"I love the water, so maybe I should open an account in the Cayman Islands. Is that how you decide? Swim or ski?" Samantha asked.

"The Swiss bankers are much more concerned about your privacy," Gary commented. "I'd do them if I were you."

"What now, Sam? Are you going to stay here for a while?" Toots asked.

"Hell, no. I want to be out of here as soon as possible." She looked at Toots and grinned.

"What?"

"I'm going to burn the house down."

119

Toots stared at her. "You're going to do what?"

"I'm gonna burn the house down. And, the barn. It all has to go."

"Why in the world do you want to do that?" Gary asked her, looking surprised.

"Because no one is going to live in this house again. Ever!" she stated emphatically.

"But..." He glanced at Toots. "What's going on?"

"Do you want to tell him?" Toots asked Samantha.

"I don't know if I should."

"It's up to you," Toots replied.

"Okay." She looked at Gary. "Can I trust you?"

"Of course," Gary told her.

Samantha stared at him, thinking about what she should do. "Okay," she said after a few moments. "Do you remember the bones we found buried by the pigsty?"

"Of course," Gary replied.

"Well, I could be wrong but I'm pretty sure those bones belong to my grandfather."

"Your grandfather, but..."

Samantha took a deep breath and let it out. "My mother was Sarah Carlson. She was John Box's granddaughter."

"Do you mean the original owner of this house?" Gary asked.

"That's right. John and his wife, Martha, only had one child. A girl. Her name was Gretchen. She married a man named Ray Slitzer. I don't know much about him, but I've heard that he wasn't a very nice man. Well, Ray disappeared in 1941. Everyone just assumed that he ran off with another woman, but... Well, I'm pretty sure that those are his bones we found buried by the pigsty."

"Why in the world would he..." Gary stopped talking as the realization of what Samantha was telling him sunk in. "Wait a minute. You're related to the man who built this house?" he asked, looking surprised.

"John Box was my great-grandfather."

"You're just full of surprises, aren't you, Sam?" Gary reached for the coffee pot and poured himself another cup of coffee. "I still don't understand why you would think that's your grandfather in the pigsty?"

Samantha got up from the table. "Wait a minute. I've got something to show you," she told him, as she walked out of the kitchen.

Gary turned to Toots. "Do you know what she's talking about?"

"Yeah, I do. Sam called me after we found those bones. If she's right, it is her grandfather out back. And, I think she's right."

"Did you know that her great-grandfather built this place?"

"I've known it longer than Sam has. You know that Sam's family and my family go way back, Gary."

"Well, shouldn't we call the police or someone?"

Toots looked at him and shook his head. "Do you seriously think we should ask the police to come here with all this money sitting here?"

"No, of course, I don't. It's just that I don't like the idea of someone being buried out there."

"I want you to look at these," Samantha said, as she came back into the room. She placed three pictures on the table. "What do you see?"

Gary studied the pictures and looked over at Samantha. "The man in this picture is wearing the belt buckle we found," he declared, holding up the picture.

"At least, it looks the same."

"It's the same buckle. See, he's wearing it in this picture, too. That man is Ray Slitzer," Samantha said.

Toots reached over and picked up one of the pictures. "This is Gretchen, isn't it?"

"That picture was taken on Gretchen's and Ray's wedding day."

"She was beautiful."

"Look closely at her fingers," Samantha told him.

"What am I looking for?" Toots asked.

"Wait," Samantha said, as she opened a cabinet drawer and pulled out a magnifying glass. "Take a closer look."

Toots took the magnifying glass and held it over the picture. "Well, I'll be damned. I don't believe it," he exclaimed.

"I knew I had seen that diamond ring before," Samantha told him. "I couldn't get it out of my mind, so I started going through some old pictures. The ring in the picture looks the same as the one we found. I can't figure out what it was doing in the pigsty, but I think it's the same ring."

"I think you're right," Toots said.

"You have to dig your grandfather up and give him a proper burial," Gary said. "You can't leave him there forever."

"I'm not sure if I want to do that."

"You should, Sam," Gary told her. "It doesn't seem right to leave him there. You should do it now before the ground freezes."

"For what reason? What would that accomplish?"

"You don't have to call the cops, but we could bury him out in the field someplace. At least he wouldn't be buried in pig shit. Nobody deserves that."

"Well, it seems that somebody thought that he did," Samantha stated.

"We still have the backhoe," Toots said. "It wouldn't be that big a deal to move him to a different spot. We know where his bones are. All we have to do is dig in that area until we find all the pieces."

"We may have already found all that there are to find. There's a good possibility that the pigs ate the rest of him," Gary said."

"Well, thanks for that image, Gary," Sam said sarcastically. "Like I don't have enough bad dreams already."

"Whattaya think, Sam? Should we dig up grandpa or not?" Toots asked, grinning.

Samantha took a deep breath and let it out. "You're right, Toots," she said smiling. "Let's dig up grandpa."

"And, bury him again," Gary added.

"And, then, burn the house down," Samantha added.

Chapter Twenty-one

Chief Charles Pritchard took one look at the room, turned around, ran outside, and tossed his cookies. He grabbed onto the outside stairs' railing and steadied himself. He hesitated to go back into the house. His stomach was still churning and he definitely didn't want to throw up again while he was in the house.

Coroner Angela Triggs waited a moment before she got out of her SUV, watching to see what Pritchard was going to do. After a few moments, she got out of her vehicle, grabbed her bag, and walked towards the Chief. "Are you okay? You're as white as a sheet," she asked.

Pritchard looked up at her as she approached him, shaking his head no. "It's bad, Angie. It's really bad."

"I'm sorry to hear that," she said as she walked up the few steps and entered the house. "Body?" she asked a uniformed cop who was standing in the kitchen.

He pointed to the living room. "It's bodies. You might want to put on a mask," he told her.

"Thanks." Angela took a few steps, stopped, and checked out the living room. "Ah, shit," she uttered and stepped back into the kitchen. "I'll be right back," she told the cop. "I need to suit up."

A few minutes later, Coroner Triggs, fully covered with protective gear and a face mask, walked back into the living room. Chief Pritchard was standing next to the door staring at the floor.

"What time did you get the call?" she asked.

"Around ten this morning. One of the locals was concerned because Ms. Carlson didn't answer her phone. After several tries with no answer, he decided to drive over and see if she was okay. This is what he found," the cop said, indicating the condition of the room.

"Did you touch the bodies?"

"Of course not."

"Have you gone through the rest of the house?"

"We did. Except for these two, it's clean."

Angela tried to avoid stepping in blood as she walked over to the closest body and bent down. "Male, about fifty." She inserted a thermometer into the body and waited. "Rigor mortis has set in. He has been shot in the forehead. Small gauge, I'd say," she told Pritchard. She pulled out the thermometer and looked at it. "Core temperature is 83.5. It looks like he's been dead for at least ten hours. I'll know more after I get him on the table."

"What about her?" Pritchard asked.

"Give me a minute, Charlie, will you?"

"Fine. I'm gonna go get some air."

"Charlie?" Angela called out.

He turned and looked at her. "What?"

"Have you called the crime scene unit yet?"

"They're on their way," he told her.

"Good. I suggest that you and your boys wait outside. Let me finish up here and we'll get these bodies out of here. Officially, they are both dead."

"Do you fucking think so?" Pritchard cried out.

Angela looked up at him. "You know I have to pronounce. I'll talk to you when I'm done here, Charlie."

Chief Pritchard turned and started to walk away.

"I'm sorry for the language, Angie. It's just that I..."

"I know. Now, get out of here. And, get your men out of here, too.

"I'll wait for you outside," he told her.

Coroner Triggs finished up with the first body and moved on to the woman. Her body core temperature was approximately the same as the man's, indicating that they had been killed around the same time. There were numerous stab wounds and when Angela turned the body on its side, she discovered that blunt force trauma had occurred to the side of her skull.

The Coroner finished doing her initial examination of the bodies, recorded her findings, and walked out of the house. She pulled off her mask and took a deep breath.

"What did you find?" Chief Pritchard asked her.

"The male was shot once. The female had her head bashed in and was stabbed repeatedly. Her face has been severely mutilated. From my experience, I'd say it was personal. Someone hated this woman. From the lack of wounds on the man, I'd say he was probably just in the wrong place at the wrong time."

"How many stab wounds did you find on the female?"

"I stopped counting at twenty but there are more. I'll give you a detailed report after I do the autopsies."

"Thanks," Pritchard said.

"Do you know who they are, Charlie?" she asked.

"I'm pretty sure that the female is Samantha Carlson. She owns the house. She hasn't lived here very long and I don't know much about her." He choked up, barely able to speak. "Christ, I'm not sure it is her," he muttered. "How could anyone know who it is? Her face is almost gone."

"I'm sorry, Charlie. I know this is hard."

"Things like this aren't supposed to happen here in Columbus. We're just a small, quiet town where everyone looks out for each other. How the hell could this happen?"

"What about the male? Do you know who it is?"

Chief Pritchard wiped his nose with the back of his hand. "Sorry, Angela. I'm acting like a baby."

"Forget it. You have nothing to apologize for. Do you know the man?"

"I don't personally know him, but Mark told me that a guy named Gary was visiting. He met him once. He said that he was Samantha Carlson's cousin."

"And, who is Mark?"

"Mark Starckweather. He's a realtor here in town. He found the bodies."

She handed Pritchard a wallet. "I found this on the body," she told him. "His driver's license says that his name is Gary Handler. He has a Chicago address. The woman is probably Samantha Carlson, but I'll need to confirm it."

"I know, but it's her. It's Ms. Carlson. Mark was positive," Pritchard told her.

"I need to call for a pickup of the bodies. Or, have you done that already?"

"No."

She turned and looked behind her. "The crime scene unit is here. Are you up to talking to them?"

"Do I have a choice?" Pritchard muttered. "God, I hate this part of the job."

"I know. Just thank your lucky stars that this isn't an everyday occurrence."

Chapter Twenty-two

"I saw Samantha last Saturday. She invited me over for dinner. We grilled a couple of steaks, had dinner together, and I left her house around nine o'clock."

"What time did you get to her house?" Pritchard asked him.

"It was around six-thirty."

"And, this cousin of hers..." Pritchard glanced down at his notes. "Her cousin, Gary Handler, showed up at what time?"

"I'm not exactly sure. The steaks were just about ready. It must have been around seven-thirty. Yeah, that sounds right. He got there just when we were about to eat."

"You said that Ms. Carlson was upset when he arrived. Why was that?"

"I guess he wasn't supposed to be there until Sunday or Monday. I don't recall which. Anyway, she wasn't happy about him showing up early."

"How long have you and Ms. Carlson been dating?"

"Oh, no," Mark said, surprised at the question. "We were just friends. Nothing more than that. Samantha hasn't lived..." He looked away. "Samantha only lived here for a few months. She didn't know anyone, so once in a while we would get together and share a meal or a glass of wine and talk."

"Do you drink a lot, Mr. Starckweather?" County Detective Sergeant Benjamin Battoon, who was sitting in on the interview, interjected.

Mark shook his head no. "Of course not."

"Did Ms. Carlson have a drinking problem?"

"Not that I'm aware of. Besides, what does having a few drinks have to do with this?" Mark asked, starting to get upset.

"I'm trying to establish habits, that's all," Battoon told him.

"What did Mr. Handler do while you were having dinner with Ms. Carlson?" Pritchard asked.

"He joined us for dinner."

"So, he was an uninvited guest. Did that upset you?" Chief Pritchard asked him.

"Not in the least. It upset Samantha though."

"Why would that upset her? After all, he was her cousin."

"I think she wanted to spend a nice evening with me and Gary could be a little obnoxious," Mark replied.

"I thought this was the first time you met him," Battoon remarked.

"It was. He just came across that way," Mark said.

"You know what I think happened, Mark? I think you were the one who was upset because when you showed up for dinner, he was already there. You had a big night planned, didn't you? You were gonna have a nice steak dinner, a few glasses of wine, and finish the night with some real hot sex. But, he spoiled that, didn't he?" Battoon sat back in his chair and glared at Mark. "So, what happened next? Did you fume about it, getting more upset every day, and then decide to have it out with him? You were gonna show him who was boss, weren't you? You were gonna teach him not to rain on your parade."

Mark stared at him, shaking his head no.

"So, you go over there and you get into a big fight and you shoot him. You planned to kill him all along, didn't you? Why else would you have a gun? Now, you have to kill Samantha. She's a witness. You took your time with her, though, didn't you? Did you rape her before you cut her face off?" Battoon stared at Mark. "Well, did you, you sick pervert?" he shouted.

"Charlie, what's he talking about? I didn't..."

"Hold on, Mark." Chief Pritchard stood up and looked at Battoon. "Could I talk to you in private?" he asked.

Battoon shrugged. "Sure. What's up?"

Mark was scared. His body was shaking. He took a sip of water and wondered what would happen if he tried to walk out. The two men were treating him like a suspect and he was getting more scared by the second. Should he yell 'lawyer' like they do in the movies? He closed his eyes and sat back in his chair. "Shit," he muttered and opened his eyes. The picture of Samantha and Gary on the floor covered with blood kept popping into his head. He wondered if he would ever be able to close his eyes again without seeing that image. How does a person deal with what he had seen this morning?

He looked up when the two men came back into the room and sat down across from him. "Are we about done here, Charlie?" he asked Chief Pritchard. "I've been here for hours. You've asked the same questions over and over. I've told you everything I know and I want to go home."

"I'm just about done, Mark," Pritchard said.

"And, what about you?" Mark asked looking at

Battoon. "Are you just about done, too?"

"Right now, I'm only here as an observer," Battoon told him.

"You could have fooled me," Mark said sarcastically.

"Did you see or talk to Samantha after you left her house Saturday night?" Pritchard inquired.

"I talked to her on Sunday."

"What was the reason for that call, Mark?" Pritchard asked.

"She called me. She wanted to apologize for her cousin's behavior the night before."

"What kind of behavior? What did he do?"

"Behavior is probably the wrong word," Mark said. "She told me that Gary was sorry that he arrived a day early and he wanted to apologize for interrupting our evening. That's all."

"I see. So, Sunday was the last time you talked to her?"

"That's right."

"I'll be checking your phone, you know."

"Check all you like. That's all you'll find, Charlie. Now, may I please go home? I'm tired and I want to take a shower and go to bed."

"That's it for now. Just make sure you stick around town in case I have further questions."

"What about my shoes?"

"We'll be keeping them for further testing."

Mark stared at him. "For what? You know I stepped in blood."

"It's just routine, Mark. Don't worry about it."

"Am I a suspect, Charlie?" he shouted. "You've known me all your life. Do you think I could do what

131

was done to Samantha? A monster did that. Not me, Charlie. I can't close my eyes without seeing her laying there in a pool of blood. And, without a face, for God's sake. How could you think that I could be capable of that?" He put his hands over his face and started to cry. "How am I supposed to be able to sleep again, Charlie? Tell me. How do I get that picture out of my head?"

Chief Pritchard looked away. "I'm sorry, Mark. I don't know what to tell you."

"Well, if it was me," Detective Sergeant Battoon told him, "I'd go home and get shit-faced."

Chapter Twenty-three

Sven Petersen grabbed the edge of the table to steady himself. "Dear God, no. When did this happen?"

Joyce, his wife, lowered the newspaper she was reading, looked at him, and listened intently.

"I'll be there this afternoon," Sven told the caller. "No, not that I know of." He listened for a moment. "She was like a daughter to us. My wife and I are... We're the closest thing she had to a family." He pulled out a chair and sat down. "I can't believe this. I'm sorry, what was that?" He glanced at the calendar hanging on the wall. "I just saw her a week ago. Can't we discuss this when I get there?" He waited for a moment. "No." He glanced over at Joyce. "Yes, I know he was there. He was helping her with some projects," he replied, as tears started rolling down his cheeks. "No, they weren't related," he said.

"Did something happen to Sam?" Joyce asked.

Sven held up his hand. "Wait," he mouthed. He shook his head, agreeing with what the caller was telling him. "Fine. I'll be there as soon as I can." He ended the call and looked at Joyce. "I don't..."

"Something happened to Sam, didn't it?"

"And, Gary." He took his wife's hand and held it. "They were murdered, Joyce. Somebody killed them."

"No!" Joyce wailed. "You're wrong. They can't be dead, Toots. They just can't be."

"Mr. Petersen, thank you for coming so soon."

"Where are they?" Sven asked Chief Pritchard as

he walked into the interview room of the police station.

"Please, sit down. Can I get you anything? Would you care for some coffee or a soft drink?"

"I'm good. Where are Sam and Gary?"

"Mr. Petersen, I'd like you to know how very sorry I am for your loss."

"Thank you. Call me Toots."

Pritchard looked surprised. "That's an unusual nickname for a man."

"Maybe, but I've been called Toots since high school."

"Well, Toots, this is a horrible thing that has happened and we are doing our best to find out who did it. The Columbia County Sheriff's Department is working very closely with us. If you don't mind, I'd like to ask Detective Sergeant Battoon to sit in with us."

"That's fine. Whatever. Can we just get on with it?"

Pritchard walked over to the door and opened it. "Ben, would you like to join us?" he called out.

Battoon walked into the room, acknowledged Chief Pritchard, and took a seat.

"Toots, I'd like you to meet Detective Sergeant Battoon from the Columbia County Sheriff's Department. Ben, this is Mr. Sven Petersen, but he prefers to be called Toots," he told Battoon, grinning.

"Do you find that amusing, Chief Pritchard?" Toots asked.

As fast as it had appeared, the grin disappeared. "Sorry. Of course not." He glanced down at a folder on the table, opened it, and studied the top sheet of paper. "Let me fill you in with what we know so far. Of course, this isn't written in stone, but we feel this is what probably happened. Ms. Carlson and Mr. Handler were murdered around midnight on Wednesday night. We received a phone call from Mark Starckweather around ten a.m. Thursday morning, telling us that he had found two bodies out at the Box House. Sorry, at Ms. Carlson's property. We still call it the Box House around here. Anyway, we arrived on the scene..."

Twenty minutes later, Toots excused himself and headed for the washroom. He stood over the sink, trying not to get ill. He turned on the cold water faucet and splashed cold water on his face. He took a deep breath, grabbed a paper towel, patted his face dry, and walked back to the interview room.

"Are you okay," Battoon asked him.

"I'm fine. It's just a lot to take in, that's all."

"Just for the record and to get it out of the way, could you tell me where you were Wednesday night?"

Toots stared at him. "You're kidding."

"It's just for the record."

"Well, just for the record and to get it out of the way, let me clarify the fact that I was in Chicago in my bed asleep. My wife will verify that. My phone will verify that. I had nothing to do with Sam's and Gary's murders and if that is the direction you're taking this..."

"No, no. I don't consider you a person of interest, Mr. Petersen," Pritchard interrupted. "I have to ask, that's all."

"Could you tell me where the bodies are? We need to make arrangements for their funerals."

"They've been taken to Portage. That's where the county morgue is."

"For autopsies?" Toots asked.

135

"Yes."

"When will the bodies be released?"

"The coroner will notify us."

"I see," Toots said sighing. "I could go for a bottle of water if it's not too much trouble."

"Not at all," Pritchard told him, as he stood and walked out of the room.

"How'd you know the Carlson woman?" Battoon asked.

"Samantha and her mother lived next to us in Chicago. Sam was pretty young when they moved in. My wife and I became her surrogate grandparents. We loved that girl like she was our own blood," Toots said, wiping his eye with the back of his hand. "Sorry."

Battoon pushed a box of tissue over to him. "No need to apologize." He waited a moment while Toots blew his nose. "What about Gary Handler? How does he fit into all of this?" Battoon turned as the door opened and Chief Pritchard came back into the room.

Pritchard handed the water to Toots and sat down. "Shall we begin?"

"I was asking him about Mr. Handler," Battoon told Pritchard.

Pritchard looked at Toots. "What can you tell us about him?"

"Gary is the son of my wife's brother Roland"

"So, you're his uncle."

"Well, yes and no," Toots replied.

"Meaning what?" Pritchard inquired.

"Roland's wife had been married and had a couple of kids before he married her. One of those kids was Gary. He raised those kids like they were his. I've always considered Gary my nephew."

136

"Did you have a good relationship with Gary?" Chief Pritchard asked.

"I loved him like he was my own. Sam was the granddaughter I never had. I loved that girl. I used to wish that the two of them would hook up, but it didn't happen."

"I understand Samantha never married. Is there a reason for that?" Battoon inquired.

"Your information is wrong. Sam married a real loser years ago. When she divorced him, she took back her maiden name."

"It seems more and more women are doing that. Do you remember who she was married to?" Chief Pritchard asked.

Toots smiled for the first time since he had received the news of the murders. "His name was Wojciechowski. Albin Wojciechowski."

Chief Pritchard held back a grin. "That's quite a mouthful. Smart move taking back her maiden name."

"Do you think Mr. Woj... Do you think her ex could be responsible for these deaths?" Battoon asked Toots.

"Not unless he came back from the grave. He died about six years ago."

"Do you know if Ms. Carlson has any other relatives?" Pritchard inquired.

"No, she doesn't. It's just me and my wife."

"Yes, but you aren't blood relatives," Pritchard stated.

"Chief Pritchard, I will be taking care of everything regarding Sam. I am the executor of her Will. I know what her wishes were in the event something should happen to her. Also, except for a few charities, I am the sole beneficiary of her estate."

"I see."

"I've notified Gary's sister of his death. I believe she will be contacting you, unless you've already talked to her."

Chief Pritchard pushed a pad of paper over to Toots. "I haven't and I do need to call her. Would you write down her name and phone number? An address, too, if you have it."

Toots pulled out his phone and checked for the number. "This is her name and phone number. I don't have an address for her."

"This is fine," Pritchard told him. "You mentioned on the phone that you had recently seen Samantha. Do you remember what day that was?"

"The last time I saw her was on Sunday, the fifteenth."

"Was there any particular reason you drove all the way from Chicago to visit her?" Battoon asked.

"Gary and I were helping her with a few projects around the property. I went back home on Tuesday."

"And, Gary stayed here?" Battoon inquired.

"Yes. I believe he was planning on going back to Chicago on Thursday."

"What were these projects you were helping her with?"

"Samantha had purchased a metal detector and she was searching the property. She had gotten a couple of strong pings from the detector and wanted to know what was buried there. So, she asked us to help her out."

"Did you find anything?"

"We certainly did. A bunch of rusty old nails. So,

we covered up the hole and forgot about it."

"Mark told us that you had been digging by the barn."

Toots looked at him, waiting for a question. "So?" he finally asked.

"I've also been told that you were using a backhoe. That you rented one here in town."

Again, Toots stared at him, waiting to see what he was getting at.

"Mr. Petersen, what were you really looking for out there?" Detective Battoon asked. "I find it hard to believe that you would drive all the way here and rent a backhoe only to find a couple of rusty nails."

"Okay, you got me. I did all that because Sam was lonely and I knew she wanted some company. She didn't want to come right out and tell me that, so this was her way of getting me to come up here. If we dug a few holes and drank a few beers, so what? She was happy to have company. She realized that moving here was a mistake. She was talking about moving back to Chicago."

"What about Mr. Handler? Why was he there?"

"That was because of me. I asked Gary if he wanted to ride along. He'd been living outside the country and had just recently come back to the states. They hadn't seen each other for a few years, so I asked him to come along. No big deal."

"Are you aware that the third and fourth floors of her house have been practically destroyed?"

"They what?" Toots asked, looking surprised.

"Did you go up there while you were visiting?" Battoon asked.

"I had no reason to go up there."

"Mr. Petersen, what were you really looking for on

that farm?" Chief Pritchard asked.

"We were playing pirates and looking for buried treasure," he replied sarcastically. "Unfortunately, all we found were some rusty nails."

"I'm finding..."

"Just nails, Chief," Toots interrupted. "If Sam was looking for something in particular, she certainly never told me about it."

Battoon sat back and stared at Toots. "They were murdered for a reason, Mr. Petersen. I think you know that reason."

"Well, you're wrong. I'd like to take a look at Samantha's house."

"Absolutely not," Chief Pritchard exclaimed. "No one is allowed on the property. It's still an active crime scene."

"I thought your men were finished with the house. What else do you expect to find?"

"I don't know but we're not done looking around. There may be something there that we missed," Pritchard told him.

"Like what? You've already done a thorough search of the house. I doubt more evidence is going to magically appear." Toots stood up and headed for the door "I'll be staying at that motel on the edge of town. If you need me, you can reach me there."

"Where are you going?" Detective Battoon asked, looking up at Toots. "We're not done here."

Toots straightened his six-foot-eleven-inch body and looked down at Battoon. "Yes, we are. I've answered your questions. I don't know anything about these murders and there isn't anything else I can tell you." He turned and walked out of the room.

Chief Pritchard looked at Detective Sergeant Battoon and shrugged. "Well, what you do think?"

"I think he's hiding something. I think he knows exactly what that woman was looking for."

"He's really big, isn't he?"

"I wouldn't want to tangle with him," Battoon stated.

"Do you think we might have missed something?"

"Not a chance. My men searched that place from top to bottom," Battoon replied.

"I wonder what happened to the knife," Pritchard mumbled. He looked over at Battoon. "By the way, did you hear from the crime lab?"

"Yeah, I got the prelims."

"I got a copy, too. It didn't say much. They did find blood and body tissue on the skillet."

"Plus, fingerprints," Battoon added.

"The coroner said that was what was used to knock out Ms. Carlson. They haven't got a match on the fingerprints yet." Chief Pritchard sat back and looked up at the ceiling. "Did you know that a minister was killed in that house back in the early '80s?" he asked Battoon. "He was hit over the head with an iron skillet."

"Really," Battoon commented. "Did they ever catch the person who did it?"

"It was his wife," Pritchard told him. "Hell, she was the one who called the police and turned herself in. She got sick of his fooling around so she killed him. Plus, he liked to spank her. This town went crazy for a while, with all the media and stuff." He smiled. "I wasn't sheriff then, of course."

"How well do you know Mark Starckweather?"

"Mark? I've known him as long as I've lived in

Columbus. The Starckweathers have been here as long as the town. He's a pretty decent guy. He does a lot for the town and he's well-liked. Why do you ask?"

"I've been thinking about who would want to hurt Ms. Carlson. She didn't move here that long ago and, except for Mark, she didn't have much to do with anyone else living here. Right now, he's at the top of my list of suspects."

"It didn't have to be someone they knew, you know," Pritchard told him.

"I guess. But, I still think we should talk to him again, Charlie."

Pritchard thought for a second, then, shook his head no. "Nah, Mark didn't have anything to do with killing those two. It would be a waste of time."

"Do you have anything better to do?" Battoon asked him.

Pritchard sighed. "All right. I'll call him and ask him to stop by. But, I still think it's a waste of time."

"I think we should talk to his wife, too."

"He's not married. He was but he got divorced about a year ago."

"He still wears his wedding ring. That's kind of unusual, isn't it?

"The ring he wears was his dad's. There's no way he'd wear a ring that his ex gave him."

"Why's that? Nasty breakup?"

"That's a nice way to put it. It was pretty ugly, but since then they've tried to get along. She works for him."

Battoon looked surprised. "Really? You don't see that happening every day."

Chapter Twenty-four

Toots checked his mirrors for traffic and started to pull out of his parking spot. He hesitated, put his truck in park, and fought the desire to break down and cry. A knock on the window startled him. He glanced over and saw Chief Pritchard looking at him through the window. He wiped the tears away with the back of his hand and lowered the window.

"Are you okay in there, Mr. Petersen?" Chief Pritchard asked. "Is there something I can do for you?"

"I'm fine. I guess this is hitting me pretty hard," Toots told him. "

"It's a terrible thing for sure. Again, I'm sorry for your loss."

"Thanks, Chief. I'll see you around." Toots started his vehicle and pulled out onto the street. He had just turned right on James Street and was headed towards River Road when his phone rang. "Hey, Joyce."

"What did you find out, Toots? Did you get into the house?"

"I'm headed in that direction right now. I'm just going to drive by. I can't go in yet. The chief of police said they are still going through it, but I don't know what for."

"Did he mention finding any money?"

"Not a word was said about money. Gary's share has to be there someplace. I want to check out his car. Maybe it's in the trunk. Hell, I don't even know if his car is still at Sam's. I forgot to ask about it. Maybe the cops have impounded it."

143

"I doubt he would have put it in the car before he was ready to leave, Toots. If the cops didn't find it, it's still in the house."

"You're probably right," Toots responded.

"How are you holding up, Sweetie?"

"I'm managing. I just am having trouble wrapping my head around this. Sam and Gary are gone. How the hell could this happen?"

"Do the cops have any suspects?"

"No. At least if they do, they aren't telling me about it."

"Who could have done this? Do you think someone heard about the money and it was a robbery attempt? Do you think that Sam told that friend of hers what she was doing?"

"I'm sure that Sam didn't tell anyone about the money and I don't think it was a robbery attempt. There was no sign of forced entry and nothing was taken. Sam probably knew the person and let him in."

"Were they both shot?" Joyce asked her husband.

"Gary was. One shot to the forehead. He died instantly," he said, his voice breaking up from emotion.

"What about Sam?"

"The police think that Sam was hit in the back of the head with a heavy object as she was leading whoever showed up into the living room. The blow knocked her out but didn't kill her. Whoever did this was after Sam and may not have known that Gary was there. It looks like Gary was just in the wrong place. This was personal, Joyce. Someone had it in for Sam."

"You don't think this was about the money, then?"

"I don't think so. Sam must have pissed someone off big time for them to do this to her."

"Was she raped?" Joyce asked softly.

"No. the coroner said that rape wasn't indicated."

"Well, thank God for that. But, if the blow to the head didn't kill her, Toots – what did?"

Toots pulled over to the side of the road, trying to control his emotions.

"Toots? Are you there?"

"I'm here. They stabbed her, Joyce. Over and over and over. She has dozens of stab wounds. And, then – then, they cut up her face. They mutilated her face. How could anyone do that? My beautiful Sam is..." He pounded his fist on the steering wheel in anger. "I'm gonna kill the bastard who did this," he yelled. "I'll fucking kill him, Joyce."

"Toots, you are not okay. I'm driving up there. I'm leaving right now."

"No. Don't. There's nothing for you to do here."

"I don't want you there all by yourself. You need me and, right now, I need you."

"I'll be okay. You stay there. I don't want you driving up in the dark."

"How long do you plan on staying there?" Joyce asked.

"I'm not sure. A couple of days, maybe. I don't know when the coroner will release the bodies. Besides, I want to get into that house. I've got to find Gary's money and I don't want to leave until I do. It's there someplace."

"He might have put it back where he found it."

"You may be right. Thank God I took Sam's money with me when I left the other day."

"That's the other thing, Toots. What are we going to do with that money? We can't keep it here forever. I'm a nervous wreck with all that money in the basement."

"I'll get it out of there as soon as I get home. There are a few charities that can benefit from it. We'll figure it out. In the meanwhile, just keep people out of the basement."

"Are you sure you don't want me to come up? I miss you."

"I'll be fine. I'm going to take a drive by Sam's house and then go to the motel and rest for a while. I'm exhausted. I'm getting too old for all this crap, Joyce."

"You make sure you eat something, Toots."

"I will. You take care, Sweetie. I'll talk to you later."

Toots pulled back onto the road and continued down the road to Sam's house. He stared at the place as he drove by looking for any activity that might be taking place there, Except for Gary's car being parked in the yard, he saw no other vehicles. He figured Sam's car was in the garage.

He drove a little further down the road, made a uey, and headed to the motel. He was physically and emotionally drained. He was going to take a nap before he ventured out again.

Toots finished his dinner and pushed his plate away. He had about a half-hour or so to kill before he drove out to the house. He motioned to the waitress that he'd like some more coffee and watched as she filled his cup. "My compliments to the chef," he said, smiling. "I enjoyed that."

"Thanks, I'll tell him."

Toots took a sip of coffee. "Good coffee, too."

"Can I get you some dessert?"

"No thanks. Just the check, please."

"Are you staying at the motel across the street?" she asked Toots.

"Uh-huh."

"Are you all alone?

"Just me," Toots told her.

"She handed him a slip of paper. "Here's my phone number. Call me if you want some company."

Toots wadded up the piece of paper and dropped it into his coffee cup. "What the hell is wrong with you? I'm old enough to be your grandfather," he exclaimed.

He paid his check and left the restaurant. As he pulled out of the restaurant's parking lot, he mumbled. "Well, here goes nothing. I either get lucky or I wind up in jail.

Chapter Twenty-five

Toots turned off the truck's lights. He was about a quarter of a mile away from the entrance to Samantha's house. Most of the houses he had passed had lights on inside but he hadn't seen anyone outside and traffic was nonexistent except for his truck. He slowed down, watching the side of the road carefully so he wouldn't miss the driveway onto her property.

He had no plan except to get in and get out. According to Chief Pritchard, the premises had been thoroughly searched by the police. Toots figured there were only a few places where the money could be. One was Gary's car but he figured that was the least likely place to hide it. His best guess was what Joyce had mentioned – that Gary had kept his portion of the money where it had been found – the elevator. Who would ever think to look under the floor of an elevator? Moretti had built a false floor accessible only from underneath, which meant the elevator had to be raised off the basement floor to get at it. Toots was amazed that Sam and Gary had found it.

He pulled his truck around to the back of the house, out of the view of any passing vehicles, and parked. He grabbed a crowbar as he got out of the truck and looked around. He listened, amazed at how quiet the night was. An owl hooted and he turned and looked towards the barn.

A small chill went through him as he recalled that it had only been a few days since they had buried Sam's grandfather's bones out in the field. They had found a total of seven bones and two teeth. Sam had polished the belt buckle and placed it on top of the small grave. He wondered what she had said to the old man while he and Gary had gone back to the barn.

Toots pulled a set of keys out of his pocket as he walked to the back door of the farmhouse. He inserted one into the keyhole. Nothing happened. He tried the next key with no luck. On the next try, the key worked and the door unlocked. He swung the door open, bent down, and entered the house avoiding the yellow tape the police had placed across the door. He had been amazed the day that he had inspected the house, to find that the doors still had locks that used old-fashioned skeleton keys. *Thank God, no one changed them*, he thought, as he let himself into the house.

The basement first, he decided. He turned on a flashlight and went down the basement steps. The bottom of the elevator was showing, which meant it had been stopped on the first floor. "Looks like I just got lucky," he mumbled, as he grabbed a ladder resting against the wall. He placed it under the elevator, climbed up a few steps, and went to work.

Deputy Monroe hung up the phone and glanced over at Chief Pritchard. "That was old lady Benson. She said that someone is messing around on the Carlson property," he told his boss.

"Right now?"

"She said she saw a pickup truck go up the drive a few minutes ago. Do you want to go check it out?"

Pritchard thought for a moment. "You sure she said a truck?"

"That's what she said."

"Yeah, go check it out. Give me a call if somebody's out there."

"You're not coming?"

"No. I've got something else I need to do."

Monroe looked at Pritchard, wondering what he was up to. "All right then. I'm outta here. Are you gonna be gone long?"

"Nope. I'll be back in a few minutes."

"Joyce, it's me. Call me as soon as you get this message."

Toots ended the call and concentrated on his driving. He certainly didn't want to get pulled over for some dumb thing. Especially, with three million dollars packed into a couple of plastic bags on the floor in the back seat. "I'd have a little trouble explaining that," he said, smiling. He jumped when his cell rang. "Shit! My nerves are shot." He glanced at his phone and let it ring. It was Joyce returning his call.

Ten minutes later he pulled into a parking spot at the motel and called Joyce. "Hi, I've got it."

"No problems?"

"None. In fact, it was almost too easy. I'm not sure what to do right now," he told her. "I can't take it into the motel and I don't want to leave it in the truck."

"Why don't you come home? You don't have to stay there."

"I don't think I should do that. It might look a little strange after I told the cops that I would be here for a few days. However..."

"What?" Joyce prompted.

"I could take it to Rockford and leave it at

Fanny's. I could be there and back here in a few hours."

"I think your sister is out of town. Didn't she say something about going to New York for a few days?"

"I know, but I can hide it in her house. I've got a key."

"Do you know the code for the alarm?"

"I do, unless she's changed it."

"Why don't I call her and give her a heads up? I'll check to see if the alarm code is the same, too."

"Why don't you do that? At least that way she'll know I've been there," he told her.

Toots ended the call and hesitated for a moment, deciding if he should run to his room and use the john before he left. His bladder made the decision for him and he jumped out of his truck and headed into the motel.

Chief Pritchard drove to the motel and pulled into the parking lot. He checked out the vehicles that were parked there, looking for Sven Petersen's truck. "There you are," he uttered when he saw the truck parked on the end. "Well, at least I know where you are."

As he turned his vehicle around and pulled back onto the street, Toots walked out of the motel. His heart skipped a beat as he noticed the police car driving away. He waited a few moments and watched the car make a left turn and speed away. "I'm sure glad I took that piss," he said to himself.

"Was there a car out there?" Pritchard asked as he answered his phone.

"False alarm. Nobody's been here," Deputy Monroe told him.

"Did you check the house?"

"Yep. The tape's still in place. Everything looks just like it did when we finished up. Maybe someone turned around in the driveway."

"I'm close to Culver's. Do you want something?"

"Nah. Wife says I need to lose a few pounds."

"I'm getting a shake. You sure I can't bring you something?"

"Nah, I'm good."

"I'll see you back at the station in a few minutes."

"Right. Over and out."

Pritchard shook his head, smiling. "You're not on a two-way radio, Al. It's a phone. You just say goodbye, not over and out."

"Sorry, Chief. Old habits, I guess."

Chapter Twenty-six

"Do I need to call Karl?"

"You don't need a lawyer," Chief Pritchard told him. "Well, you don't unless you have something to hide. I only want to go over a few things with you, Mark. You knew Samantha Carlson better than anyone in town. I need your help. I'm hoping you can throw some light on this situation."

"I don't know what I could tell you that you don't already know."

"Tell me again why you went over to her house so early in the morning."

"It was ten o'clock. That isn't early, Charlie. And, I already told you why."

"Humor me. Tell me again."

"I drove over there because Samantha wasn't answering her phone. I was concerned that something might have happened to her."

"Like what?"

Mark shrugged. "I don't know. She could have fallen or was sick. I was just concerned, that's all."

"Why were you calling in the first place? What was it you wanted to talk to her about?"

"Her cousin Gary. Well, he wasn't her cousin, was he? I know that now. I wanted to ask her how long Gary would be staying with her. I wanted to ask her out – you know, for dinner – but, I didn't want Gary to come along. So, I figured I'd set something up for after he left."

"You didn't like the guy?"

"Not really. He had this attitude like he was so much better than everyone else."

"So, he got on your nerves? Made you angry?"

"Yeah, he got on my nerves, but I didn't kill him. Or, Samantha."

"Why do you think Samantha passed him off as her cousin? Do you think something was going on between the two of them?"

"I don't know why she did that. Maybe, she was embarrassed that he showed up unexpectedly and it was the easiest way to explain him being there. I know she expected him the following day." He hesitated. "Maybe it was Monday. I'm not sure." He shrugged. "Anyway, I have no idea if anything was going on."

"Did you have feelings for Samantha, Mark?"

Mark looked away. He closed his eyes, took a deep breath, and let it out. "I liked her. A lot. But, I didn't see it going beyond being friends. She didn't give off that vibe, you know?"

"What vibe is that?" Chief Pritchard asked.

"You know. Those flirty things women do... Body language, I guess you call it. She didn't come across that she wanted anything more than to be friends."

"What about you? Did you want to be more than friends?"

Mark gave him a questioning look. "What are you getting at, Charlie?"

"You must see how this looks, Mark. You have the hots for Samantha and she doesn't give you the time of day. Then, this Gary guy shows up and you figure something is going on between them. You leave, all pissed off because you think she's sleeping with him. The idea that the two of them are having sex eats at your brain until you decide to have it out with her."

"Are you fucking kidding me?" Mark stared at Pritchard. "You're nuts, Charlie. You're one hundred percent certifiably nuts."

"You get in your car and drive over to her house," Pritchard continued, ignoring Mark's comment. "She lets you in. But, she's not happy that you're there. She yells at you – screams at you – and you hit her. She falls and hits her head on the edge of the coffee table. Or, maybe you hit her with something. Suddenly, Gary rushes towards you, trying to protect Samantha, and you shoot him. Samantha looks up at you from where she is laying on the floor and..." Pritchard thought for a second. "She screams, doesn't she? You want to shut her up, so you get a knife from the kitchen and you stab her. Over and over and over. You don't stop until you're so exhausted you can barely raise your arm. There's blood everywhere. You're covered with it. You drop the knife, scared now as the reality of what you've just done starts to set in. You've just killed two people. You panic. Your heart is beating so fast that you think you're having a heart attack. You've got to get out of there."

Mark's mouth drops open in disbelief as he listens to Chief Pritchard. He shakes his head back and forth in denial. "What the hell is wrong with you? You sound just like... Like Battoon," he yelled at Pritchard.

"Then, what happened, Mark? Did she cry out for help? Maybe plead with you to help her? She's supposed to be dead. Why isn't she dead? Incensed now, you pick up the bloody knife and you stab her one more time. Only this time you take your time. You plunge the knife into her chest, sit back, and watch her slowly die." Chief Pritchard sat back and stared at Mark. "One thing I don't understand, though," he said softly. "Why did you mutilate her face?" Suddenly, he pounded the table with his fist. "Tell me!" he yelled.

Mark jumped, fighting to control his bladder. "I want an attorney," he said, his voice shaking. "I want to call Karl."

Chief Pritchard stood up and started pacing the room. "You don't need to call anyone. You're not under arrest. I know you didn't do it. But, you see how it looks, don't you? This is very close to Detective Sergeant Battoon's version of what happened, Mark."

Mark glared at him. "You son of a bitch, Charlie. How could you do that to me?"

"That's just a sample of what Battoon will do if he gets the chance. You're his only suspect and he's pretty much made up his mind that you did it."

Mark took a long swallow of water. "Well, then he better find another suspect 'cause I'm not taking the rap for this."

Chief Pritchard sat back down and looked across the table at Mark. "We're expecting the forensics to give us something. We found fingerprints on that skillet."

"Well, they weren't mine."

"More coffee?" Pritchard asked him.

"No. Thanks. That was a shitty thing you did, Charlie. My heart's still pounding."

"I know, but I wanted you to be prepared in case that a-hole Battoon comes after you."

"There must be a hundred different ways you could have done it."

"Did Samantha ever say why she bought that house?" Pritchard asked, changing the subject.

"I've wondered about that, too. She never opened

156

up much about herself. I always had the feeling that it was personal."

"So, she never mentioned what brought her to Columbus?"

"Nope. Not that I recall."

"You met Sven Petersen, didn't you?"

"Oh, yeah. You don't forget meeting him," Mark said grinning. "He's one big mutha, isn't he?"

"That he is. You don't think he had anything to do with the killings, do you?"

Mark shook his head no. "He loved her like a daughter. And, it was mutual. And, Gary was his nephew. No, I'd rule Toots out for sure."

"Toots. What the hell kind of a nickname is that?"

Mark smiled. "I know. Right? Do you know he's six-eleven? He told me he had shrunk an inch."

"He's in town, you know," Charlie told him.

"It's understandable. He was her only family, you know. He and his wife."

"Poor guy got hit with a double wammy, losing both of them like that."

"Are we done here?" Mark asked.

"For now. I'll try to keep Battoon away from you."

"Thanks."

"How are you and Gloria doing?" Pritchard asked grinning.

Mark rolled his eyes. "I'd fire her if I could. She drives me nuts."

"What's stopping you?"

"The divorce agreement. The biggest mistake I ever made is agreeing to let her work for me."

Pritchard looked confused. "Why did you do that? She almost drove you crazy while you were married to her and, then, you agree to let her work for you. It doesn't make a whole lot of sense, Mark."

"It was only for two years. Money was tight when we got divorced. I couldn't afford to pay her alimony and she couldn't find a job. So, instead of paying someone else to run the office, I agreed to let her work for me. I figured I could put up with her for a couple more years. Anyway, it will be over in another year."

"How's that working out?" Pritchard said grinning.

"Not funny, Charlie." He sighed. "She eavesdrops on my conversations, thinks I want to sleep with every woman client I have, goes through my drawers when I'm not there, and..."

"What?"

"Nothing. Sorry I went off like that."

"What were you going to say, Mark?"

"Well, it's because of her that I haven't dated much since the divorce. If Gloria gets wind of me seeing someone – even for an innocent dinner – she goes crazy. So, I stay away from the women here in town, which pretty much leaves me dating Rosey Palm and her five sisters."

Pritchard laughed. "I remember those days. Anyway, you knew what she was like when you made that deal. I can't say I feel sorry for you."

"I'm not looking for sympathy, Charlie. But, sometimes trying to save a buck or two can cost you an arm and a leg." He grinned. "And, your sanity."

"Did she know that you had a relationship with Samantha Carlson?"

"Probably. And, I told you it wasn't a relationship. Samantha and I were only friends."

"I know what you said. Do you think Gloria is

capable of murder?”

“God, no,” Mark said, surprised Pritchard would suggest such a thing. “Are you serious?”

“Right now, I’m not ruling out anyone. But, I’m pretty sure we’re looking for a man. You’re good to go. Thanks for coming in, Mark.”

“Thanks for the heads up about Battoon. I’ll be sure to bring Karl along if he wants to question me.”

“Good idea.”

Pritchard waited until Mark left the police station before he picked up the phone and made a call.

“Hello. This is Chief of Police Charles Pritchard from the Columbus, Wisconsin Police Department. I’m looking for some background information on a woman named Samantha Carlson. She recently moved here from Chicago. Are you the person I need to talk to?”

Chapter Twenty-seven

Chief Pritchard finished reading Samantha's autopsy report. His stomach was a little queasy and he wished he hadn't eaten breakfast that morning.

Deputy Monroe looked up from his desk. "Did you say something?"

"Samantha Carlson was stabbed twenty-seven times."

"Talk about overkill."

"Damn, that's a lot of anger," Pritchard declared.

"What about Gary Handler?"

"A single gunshot wound to the forehead. The coroner didn't find any other wounds or bruising."

"Well, he got lucky, if you can call it that. I still have trouble closing my eyes at night since I saw that crime scene," Monroe told him. "How could anyone do that to another person?"

"It takes all kinds, Al."

"It had to be premeditated, don't you think? Otherwise, why bring a gun?" Monroe asked.

"And, why not shoot both of them? We'll probably never know what happened unless we get a confession from the killer. Well, I guess I better call Toots and let him know that the bodies have been released."

"He'll be glad to hear that. I imagine he doesn't want to stay here any longer than necessary." He grinned as the phone rang. "Maybe, that's him now."

"Columbus Police, Chief Pritchard." He listened carefully to the caller. "Are you sure?" He shook his head up and down. "Got it. Will you email me a copy of those?" He made some notes on a pad of paper and frowned. "I see. When will you know?" He waited a few seconds. "When?" he asked, looking surprised. "All right. Thanks for letting me know."

Deputy Monroe waited for Pritchard to say something. "Who was that?" he finally asked.

"That was the lab,"

"I gathered that. What did they say?"

"The skillet is definitely what was used to hit Samantha Carlson on the back of the head. The lab found tissue and blood on it."

"We already knew that," Monroe stated. "What else?"

"There were numerous fingerprints found that they haven't been able to identify. I need to bring Toots in and take his prints for comparison. He was in that house more than once, so some of those prints could be his."

"You already took Mark's prints, so they can rule him out," Monroe said.

"The fingerprints that were on the skillet don't match any prints they have on file. And, they didn't get any DNA off of the bodies."

"And, we don't have any suspects." He looked at Pritchard. "We don't, do we?"

"Agent Battoon thinks Mark did it," Pritchard said.

"What?" Monroe exclaimed, looking surprised. "No way in hell Mark did it. Battoon's crazy if he thinks Mark had anything to do with those murders."

"I agree. I doubt it's anyone from around here."

"If you had to pick someone who you think could have done this, who would it be?" Monroe asked.

Pritchard looked surprised. "You mean from Columbus?"

"Yeah, from Columbus."

Pritchard shook his head. "I have no idea. I mean, we've got some real looney people living here, but murder? I don't know. What about you?"

"Gloria Starckweather."

"You're not serious?" Pritchard asked, surprised at Monroe's answer.

"Totally. I think she's capable of it. Everyone in town knows she's a little crazy plus jealous as shit. If she thought for one minute that Mark was messing around with Samantha Carlson... Well, let's just say that I wouldn't want to be Samantha Carlson."

"It took a lot of strength to do what was done to Carlson. I don't know if a woman could do that."

"Gloria is pretty fit, Charlie. She works out at that women's gym. Besides, you've heard of women doing unbelievable things when that adrenaline kicks in. I think she could do it."

"Well, she's not a suspect and let's not be making one up." Pritchard picked up a sheet of paper and glanced at it. "By the way, I've got the Chicago police digging into Samantha Carlson's past. Hopefully, they'll come up with something that will help us. Until then, Al, I'm at a dead end."

"Maybe somebody who saw or heard something that night will still come forward."

"I'm not holding my breath for that to happen. Besides, if someone saw something, we'd know about it by now." He stood up and stretched. "God, my neck is stiff. I must have slept really crooked last night," Pritchard said. "I'm going to go talk to Sven Petersen.

Hold down the fort"

Pritchard pulled into the motel's parking lot and looked for Toot's truck. He noted that it was parked in the same spot as it had been the night before. He parked his squad car and called Petersen.

"What's up, Chief?"

"Are you decent? I'm out front and I'd like to talk to you for a few minutes."

"Is everything okay?"

"Everything is fine."

"Give me a sec. I'll meet you downstairs," Toots said.

Toots shook Chief Pritchard's hand and sat down. "So, what brings you by?"

"I heard from the coroner's office this morning. They've completed the autopsies."

"So, I can have the bodies transported back to Chicago?"

"That's right."

"Well, that's a relief."

"Again, Toots, I'm sorry for all of this."

"I take it that you're done with the house, too."

Chief Pritchard thought for a moment. "I guess we are. I'll have Deputy Monroe drive over there and take the tape down."

"Thanks. I want to pick up a few of Samantha's things before I go back to Chicago. Gary's stuff, too. Do you have a key to the house you can give me?"

"You don't have one?"

"Sam never gave me one."

"I have her keys at the station. You can pick them

up there."

"Thanks."

"There's one other thing, Toots. I need to take your fingerprints. It's strictly for elimination. We have several prints we're trying to match and..."

"No problem," Toots said, interrupting Pritchard. "I'd be glad to help."

"Thank you."

"I'll probably be driving back home tonight. I've got a few calls - arrangements to make before I check out of here. I can stop by the station after that and pick up the keys, if that's okay?"

"That works. We'll take your prints when you come by. I think I should warn you, Toots. Samantha's house hasn't been cleaned. I'm not sure you want to go in there. Maybe, you should think about it."

"I've probably seen worse," Toots said, surprising Chief Pritchard.

"Really?"

"I was a Chicago cop before I went into the construction business. There's not much I haven't seen."

"You're an ex-cop? I never would have guessed it."

"For twenty years."

"Why'd you retire?"

"I had my years in and I'd had enough of the bullshit. Being a cop in Chicago is a lot different than being one in a small town. It's pretty political and more who you know than what you know. Anyway, a couple of us cops decided to open a small construction company. It took off and we did pretty good. I still work at it now and then, but I'm mostly retired."

"It sounds like it all worked out for you."

"Pretty much. Do you have any crime scene cleaners around here? I'm going to have to get that place cleaned up and eventually put it on the market."

"I think you might have to go as far as Milwaukee to find people who do that kind of work. Maybe, Madison has a few. I'm not sure, Toots, but, I can check it out for you."

"Nah, that's all right. I'll take care of it. But, thanks, anyway."

"I'll get going, then. I'll see you at the station," Pritchard said

"I should be there in an hour or so," Toots told him.

Chapter Twenty-eight

Toots walked out of the police station and turned right. Starckweather Realty was a couple of stores away and he wanted to talk to Mark.

Gloria looked surprised. "Whoa! You're a tall drink of water, aren't you?" she commented, grinning.

Toots smiled. "So, I've been told. Is Mark here?"

"I'm sorry, he's out right now. Is there something I can help you with?"

"When will he be back?"

"I'm not sure," she told him.

"Why not?" Toots asked her.

"I'm sorry. Why not what?"

"You work here, don't you? Shouldn't you know where your boss is and when he'll be back?"

Gloria smiled at him. "I'm sorry, but it doesn't work like that here. I'm never quite sure when he's gonna pop in. All I know is that right now he's taking pictures of a house that we're listing. I have no idea how long it's going to take him or if he's coming back here at all."

"Can you call him?"

"I can only call him if it's an emergency."

"It's an emergency. Call him and tell him I need to talk to him before I leave town."

"I'm sorry. But, who are you?"

"Just tell him Toots wants to talk to him."

Gloria smiled. "I should have known it was you, Mr. Petersen. Mark mentioned he'd met you. He said you were quite tall. He certainly wasn't exaggerating."

Toots stared at her.

"Is there something else?" Gloria asked, starting to get nervous.

"Are you gonna call him?"

"I'm sorry. Of course, I am." She grinned. "He's going to be so pissed that I'm disturbing him. Isn't that great?"

"Why would pissing him off be great?" Toots asked, staring down at her.

"Never mind, you wouldn't get it." She picked up the phone and called Mark.

Mark Starckweather stormed into the office, madder than hell. "You know you're not supposed to call me when I'm in the middle of a listing. What the hell is so important that it couldn't wait?" he yelled.

"Don't you yell at me!" she shouted.

"Where is he?" Mark asked, looking around the office.

"He's in the washroom and quiet down, will you?"

Mark turned as the washroom door opened and Toots walked out. "I'm sorry to bother you, Mark, but I have some business I'd like to discuss with you. I'm heading back to Chicago and I wanted to talk to you before I leave."

"What business?" Mark asked, looking troubled.

"It's about the farm."

"What about it?"

"I'd like you to list it when it's ready to be put up for sale." He glanced towards Mark's office. "Can we talk in there?"

"Of course," Mark said, as he started to calm down. He turned to Gloria. "Hold my calls."

"Yes, boss," she replied sarcastically.

"By the way, the coroner has released the bodies," Toots told Mark.

Mark looked at him, wondering where this was going. "That's good to hear."

"We'll bury Sam next to her mother in Chicago. There's a spot there for her. I'm not sure about Gary. He has relatives in Chicago and Rockford. It's up to them. I'm still waiting to hear what they want to do." Toots looked away.

"I can't tell you how sorry I am about what happened, Toots. I liked Samantha. She was a nice person."

Toots shook his head. "Yeah, I'm sorry, too. It won't be the same without her. She was planning on moving back to Chicago, you know."

Mark looked surprised. "I didn't know that. She never said anything to me about it. I guess she wasn't happy here."

"She never planned on staying."

"I don't get it. If she wasn't planning on staying here, why'd she buy the farm in the first place?"

"A few more months – hell, maybe weeks - and she would have been out of here."

"I'm sorry to hear that," Mark said, still confused at what Toots was getting at.

Toots sighed. "Yeah, it's a shame that this happened in your town."

"Well, if there's anything I can do, please let me know. I'll be happy to list it when you're ready."

"That's good of you. So, I'm a little curious, Mark. Was there anything going on between you and Sam?"

Mark sat back in his chair and stared at Toots. "Are you asking if we ever had an affair, because that's none..."

"I want to know if you were just friends like you claim, or more than that," Toots interrupted.

"We were friends. Period! That's it. And, I'm sick of being asked that question," he shouted. "Why is it that a man and a woman can't be friends without everyone reading more into it?" He turned away from Toots, trying to hold back his emotions.

"I'm trying real hard to believe you, Mark. But, somebody from this town killed Sam and Gary. You're the only one here that she was friendly with."

Mark stood up and pointed to the door. "I don't like what you're insinuating and I'd like you to leave. I had nothing to do with those murders and I don't give a flying fuck if you believe me or not."

Toots stared at Mark, surprised at his outburst. "I'd like to think you're telling the truth."

"Of course, I'm telling the truth. I didn't hurt her or your nephew," he told him, as the tears rolled down his face. "I could have loved her if she had given me the chance. But, she only wanted to be friends. And, that is exactly what we were. Friends."

"Okay, then. I'm sorry if I upset you, but this whole thing is driving me nuts. I'll give you a call about the house," Toots said as he walked towards the door.

"Please, don't. I don't want anything more to do with that place – ever."

"Got it," Toots told him. He opened the door and practically bumped into Gloria. "Did you get all that?" he asked as he walked past her.

She looked into Mark's office and grinned. "Well,

will you look at that," she declared, looking at Toots. "You did something I could never do in all the years I was married to him."

"What's that?"

"You made that son of a bitch cry."

Chapter Twenty-nine

Sven Petersen locked up the house and got in his truck. He wished he would never have to step one foot in that house again, but he knew he had to make one more trip before all this business was over. He glanced back at the house as he drove away. "Damn house was nothing but trouble," he muttered. A tear filled the corner of his eye and he wiped it away.

He turned right out of the drive, drove down River Road to James Street, and stopped. "Shit! He exclaimed, upset that he had forgotten something. He pulled a uey and drove back to the house.

He unlocked the door to the house and ran into the bedroom where Samantha had slept. On the top shelf of the closet were two photograph albums. He grabbed them and went back outside. He locked the door once more, got into his truck, and drove away.

As he turned south on Ludington Street, he noticed Mark Starckweather walking into the police station carrying a small plastic bag.

"What's up, Mark? You sounded upset when you called."

Mark handed Chief Pritchard a plastic bag. "I found this in the trunk of Gloria's car. I'm not sure if it's anything important but I thought I should show this to you."

Pritchard opened the bag and looked inside. "Shoes?"

"Gloria's shoes, Charlie. There's blood on them."

"How do you know it's blood?"

"Well, it looks like blood to me. I guess it could be something else, though."

"Where did you say you found them?" Pritchard asked.

"They were in the trunk of her car. It's probably nothing but when I saw them, I had this weird feeling that something was off. I mean, like why would her shoes have blood on them?"

"You mean what you think is blood," Pritchard said, correcting him. "What were you doing snooping around in the trunk of her car?"

"I wasn't snooping. My car is in for an oil change, so I'm using Gloria's car today. The Bennett's put their house up for sale, and I was headed over there to put up a for-sale sign in the front yard. When I put the sign in the trunk, I noticed this bag. I got nosy and looked inside."

"So, you were snooping," Pritchard commented, grinning.

"Whatever. But, that's when I saw the blood – or whatever it is - on the shoes."

"Where's the car now?" Pritchard inquired.

"It's parked out front."

Pritchard held out his hand. "Keys."

Mark handed him the keys and started to follow him out of the police station.

Pritchard turned to him. "Stay here."

Mark watched through the window as Pritchard opened the trunk and glanced inside. Suddenly, Chief Pritchard slammed the trunk shut and walked back into the station. "Nothing there?" he asked Pritchard.

"I need gloves," Pritchard said brusquely, as he

172

walked past Mark.

"Did you find something?" Mark inquired.

Pritchard turned back to Mark. "You can leave. The car stays."

"But..."

"No buts, Mark. You need to leave. I'll let you know if we find anything of any importance."

Mark stared at him.

"Now, Mark. Go."

The luminol tests that were done on the shoes and the stains in the trunk of Gloria's car proved positive for blood. Chief Pritchard cut a square out of the carpet in the trunk of her car and put it in an evidence bag. He knew he had blood. He wasn't sure whose, but he had the sinking feeling that it would be a match to Samantha Carlson.

Pritchard was taking no chances and had decided to drive up to Portage to hand-deliver the potential evidence to the forensics department. He knew it could take twenty-four to seventy-two hours before they would know anything. In some cases, it took longer and he was hoping that they would rush this through for him.

He had impounded Gloria's car, making sure that no evidence would be compromised. He grinned. He sure wouldn't want to be in Mark's shoes when she found out her car had been impounded. That girl was famous for her nasty temper. He wouldn't be surprised if he had another murder on his hands when he got back to town.

Mark walked past Gloria and headed straight for his office. He was so nervous his hands were shaking.

173

He closed the door, locked it, and sat down behind his desk. He knew when Gloria found out her car had been impounded, all hell was gonna let loose.

He opened the bottom left drawer of his desk and reached for a bottle of whiskey. He looked confused when he picked up an empty bottle with a note attached to it. "What the hell?" he mumbled. He pulled the note off of the bottle and stared at it. *Surprise. I dumped this, just like I dumped you.*

He sat back and took a deep breath. He knew he had to cool off before he totally lost it and did something he'd regret. He closed his eyes and concentrated on his breathing. His heart rate slowly dropped back to normal and he started to feel in control again.

"Shit," he mumbled when the doorknob turned.

"Why is the door locked?" Gloria called out.

"Go away. I'm busy," he yelled.

"I'm leaving. I need my car keys."

"I don't have them. I lost them."

"Stop messing around, Mark. I want my keys."

"Seriously, I don't have them."

"Unlock the door, Mark," Gloria demanded.

"I don't think I can do that," Mark told her.

Gloria thought for a moment, went to her desk, opened a drawer, and took out a key. She walked back to Mark's office, inserted the key, and unlocked the door.

Mark stared at her as she entered the room.

"There's always more than one key to a lock, Mark. Did you really think you could hide from me? Now, give me my fucking keys."

"I'm telling you, I don't have them."

"Then, where are they? Did you honestly lose

them?"

"Chief Pritchard has them. If you want them, you'll need to talk to him."

"Why in the world does he have them?" she asked, looking confused.

Mark stared at her. "I don't know," he finally said.

"You don't know? How could you not know?"

He didn't say anything.

"Oh, for God's sake, you're as useless as tits on a bull," she said, as she turned and walked out of the room.

Mark waited until he heard the front door close. He grabbed his phone and called the auto repair shop. "Hi, Joe. It's Mark. I seem to have a transportation problem. Can one of your guys drop my car off? I'm at my office."

Chapter Thirty

Detective Sergeant Benjamin Battoon sat back in the chair and listened. So far, Chief Pritchard seemed to be asking all the right questions. He made a bet with himself that Gloria Starckweather would be in tears and confessing within the next five minutes.

"Fuck you, Charlie Pritchard. You have no idea what the hell you're talking about. I didn't even know that woman or her boyfriend. What reason would I have to kill them?"

"Gary Handler wasn't her boyfriend."

Gloria shot Pritchard a disgusted look. "I could care less what he was. I wasn't at that house and I didn't kill anyone. What the hell is wrong with you?"

"Where's the gun, Gloria?"

"What gun?"

"You know what gun. The gun you used to kill Gary Handler. What did you do with it? Did you throw it in the Crawfish River?"

Gloria looked at Pritchard and shook her head. "You've been watching too much TV." She looked down at her hands. "I need a manicure," she mumbled to herself. She glanced up at Pritchard. "By the way, when am I going to get my car back?"

Chief Pritchard looked over at Battoon. "She doesn't get it, does she?"

Battoon leaned forward and stared at Gloria. "Mrs. Starckweather, do you understand that you are about to be arrested for a double homicide?"

"What I understand, you fucking moron, is that

176

you don't have a shred of evidence that I was anywhere near that house the night those two people were killed. What you have is a pair of tennis shoes which I haven't worn in over a year, with some blood on them. Anyone could have put those shoes in my trunk, but it sure as hell wasn't me."

"We also found blood in your trunk, Gloria. Samantha Carlson's blood. How do you explain that?"

"It's easy. Whoever is trying to frame me for those murders put it there."

"Why would someone do that?"

"Well, I imagine so he could take the suspicion off of himself. My God, man, do I have to do your job for you?"

"Every person in town knows how jealous you are of Mark. You've never gotten over the fact that he divorced you. He was friends with Samantha and you couldn't stand it. I don't think you planned to kill Gary Handler. You probably didn't even know he was going to be there, did you? Tell us what happened, Gloria. Did he attack you and you had to shoot him to protect yourself?"

Gloria shook her head. "You are so wrong."

"We know you did it, so why not tell us exactly what happened?" Battoon told her. "Make it easy on yourself."

Gloria sat back in her chair and smiled. "I'm tired of this. Am I under arrest?"

Pritchard glanced over at Battoon, who shook his head yes. "Yes, you are," Pritchard said. "I guess I better read you your rights."

"Don't bother," Gloria told him. "I didn't do it. I wasn't even in town that night, Charlie. And, I can prove it."

"You have an alibi?" Pritchard asked her, looking surprised.

"I sure do."

"Mrs. Starckweather," Battoon said, leaning forward in his chair, "if you have an alibi, why are you just mentioning it now? We've been questioning you for over an hour. Why didn't you say something before now?"

Gloria shrugged. "I don't know. I guess I wanted to see how far you were gonna take this. You've known me forever, Charlie. How could you think I could do this?"

"It's because I've known you forever that I thought you could do this, Gloria. You've got a hell of a temper, and you're jealous as hell of Mark. I don't doubt for a moment that you're capable of doing something like this," he said raising his voice.

Gloria sat back in her chair and stared at him. "That hurt, Charlie."

"Where were you?" Battoon asked her.

She glanced over at him, looking confused.

"The night of the murders," Battoon said. "Where were you?"

"Oh, that. I was in Madison in a motel having sex." She grinned. "Some great sex, as I recall. I spent the night there. I didn't get home until around six the next morning."

"We'll need the name of the person you were with," Pritchard said, looking disappointed.

"Of course."

"And, he's going to confirm what you just told us?"

178

"He is."

I should still arrest you, Gloria."

"For what? I didn't do anything wrong."

"For wasting my time," Pritchard yelled.

"Well, at least now I know what you think of me. Thanks for that."

"Mrs. Starckweather?" Battoon said.

"What now," she snapped.

"Did Mark ever talk about his feelings for Samantha Carlson?"

Ignoring Battoon, she turned and stared at the police chief. "Charlie, who do you think put those shoes in the trunk of my car?"

"Mark told me they were in there when he opened the trunk."

She laughed. "And, you believe him?"

"I don't have a reason not to," Pritchard replied.

"God, you're such an idiot. Of course, it was Mark. Everyone knows he hates me. He'd do anything to get me out of his hair."

"Does that include framing you for murder? I find that hard to swallow, Gloria."

"I'm pretty sure he did it, Charlie. Maybe, you should take a closer look at what he was doing that night. May I leave now?"

Pritchard slid a pad of paper across the table. "Write down your friend's name and phone number," he said handing her a pen. "Then, you can leave."

Gloria wrote down the information and slid the pad back to him. "Now?"

"Go ahead. But, stay in town, Gloria. I mean it," Pritchard told her.

Gloria put the pen in her purse and stood up.

Pritchard held out his hand. "Nice try. Pen, please."

Gloria grinned and handed the pen to him. "See ya,"

"One more thing, Gloria," Pritchard called out as she headed for the door.

She turned and looked at him. "What?"

"You might want to keep this conversation between us."

"You mean don't tell Mark, don't you?"

"Yeah. If he is the one who put those shoes and blood in the trunk of your car... Well, let's keep it to ourselves. Okay?"

"I guess I can do that. By the way, when will I get my car back? I'm tired of walking everywhere."

"We'll see. I'll let you know."

Battoon sat back and sighed. "Well, that takes care of that. Our only suspect just walked out the door."

"She didn't do it, Ben. I don't doubt for a minute that her alibi will check out."

"For a while there, I thought she was going to break down and confess that she did it."

"Gloria? Never. She's a tough old broad."

"Now do you think that Mark Starckweather was the one who killed them?" Battoon asked.

"I still have trouble believing it was him. But, if he's trying to set up Gloria by putting those shoes in her trunk..." He thought for a moment. "It's only Gloria's word. We don't know that he did do that. And, we don't have any real evidence against him."

"Well, his fingerprints were in the house."

"And, that doesn't prove a thing. It's no surprise

his prints were there. He'd been in that house many times. We still don't know whose fingerprints were on that skillet. We don't have the knife that was used on Samantha and we don't have a smoking gun. In other words, we have nothing," Pritchard said emphatically.

"Do you think he put those shoes in that trunk?"

"I think he's capable of doing it," Pritchard replied. "He hates Gloria and I wouldn't put it past him to do something like that."

"But, how would he get the blood?"

"Benjamin, he has keys to every house he's ever listed in this town. It wouldn't surprise me if he crept into that house one night and rubbed Gloria's shoes in some of Samantha's blood. My God, that floor was covered with it."

Battoon stared at him. "He hates her that much? But, they work together. I don't get it."

"It's only because they have to." Pritchard stood up and stretched. "I think we should..." He hesitated. "Much as I hate to say it, I think we should take a closer look at Mark," he told Battoon.

"I figured it was him all along."

"God, I hope you're wrong," Pritchard said.

"We'll see. Right now, I'm going to check out Gloria Starckweather's alibi."

"Well, that takes care of that," Battoon declared, as he hung up the phone.

"She was there?" Pritchard asked.

"She was there. He said they had dinner and a few drinks, checked into the motel, and Gloria left a little before six the following morning. He stayed at the motel until around nine, had their complimentary breakfast, and checked out. It looks like her alibi is good."

"That leaves Mark."

Gloria knocked on Mark's office door.

"What now, Gloria?" he yelled.

"I'd like to talk to you for a minute."

He hesitated a moment. "All right. Come on in."

Gloria walked into his office and sat down. "I'm giving you my two weeks' notice."

Mark looked shocked. "You're what? Did I hear that right? You're quitting?"

"I am. I can't work here any longer. It's not healthy, me working here. This hate between us is bad for both of us, Mark. It's time I move on."

Mark stared at her. "I can't believe what I'm hearing. You're quitting. You're actually quitting." He grinned. "That's great, Gloria. You're right. It is time for us to move on."

She stared at him. "I haven't seen you this happy in a long time. You really do want me to leave, don't you?" she said.

"I do. I think it's for the best."

"Well, forget it, you prick!" she shouted. "Our divorce agreement says two years, buddy, and I'm not leaving one day before those two years are up. Got it? Did you really think you could get rid of me by throwing a bloody pair of shoes in my trunk?"

Marked glared at her. "You bitch. Get out of my office."

Gloria smiled and stood up. "I'm going to lunch."

"Go. And, don't bother to come back," he said, holding out his hand. "I want the keys to the office. You're fired."

Chapter Thirty-one

"Do you think we'll ever find out who killed them?" Deputy Monroe asked. "It's been almost two months since they were murdered."

"I know how long it's been, Al. You don't have to keep reminding me. I go through the file almost every day to make sure we didn't miss something."

"Sorry, but I still have bad dreams about it." He held up the coffee pot. "Do you want some more?"

"Nah, I've had enough," Pritchard told him, as he leafed through a pile of papers on his desk. "I'm looking for the name of that guy that Gloria was with that night. Was it Frankel? Fielding?" He looked at Deputy Monroe. "Do you remember his name?"

"I think it was Fuller. Did you look in the file?"

"That's it. Fuller. Patrick Fuller. Where did I put that damn file?" he mumbled, as he started moving papers around on his desk.

"What do you want that for?" Monroe asked.

"I wanna talk to Fuller again. You know, to see if his story has changed."

Deputy Monroe picked up the coffee pot and poured the rest of the coffee into his cup. "Are you done doing your Christmas shopping?"

Pritchard faked a groan. "I'm done, except for the wife. God, I never know what to get that woman. What about you?"

"I'm just about finished." Monroe sat back and stared at the ceiling. "Do you remember the name of the motel that they stayed in?" Monroe asked, changing the subject.

"Who? You mean Gloria and her boyfriend?"

"Yeah. What motel was it?"

"I don't know. It was one of those on the outskirts of town on Hwy. 151." He glanced across the room at Deputy Monroe. "What do you want to know that for?"

"Well, I'm trying to remember if anyone checked with the motel. I mean, that Fuller guy said he was with Gloria that night but did anyone check with the motel and confirm it?"

"Yeah, Battoon did." He thought for a few seconds and frowned. "He did, didn't he? Shit, where's that damn file?"

"Look in the bottom tray."

"Found it," Pritchard said. He opened it and flipped through the pages until he found the report on Gloria Starckweather. "Well, I'll be damned," he exclaimed. "There's no mention of Agent Battoon ever talking to anyone from the motel, Al."

"Do you want me to call 'em and find out?" Deputy Monroe asked. "They should be able to pull that information up on their computer."

"I'll do it."

Twenty minutes later, Chief Pritchard ended the call to the motel in Madison. "We need to pick up Gloria," he told Deputy Monroe.

"Yeah, I heard," Monroe said. "It was her all along, wasn't it?"

"It looks like it," Pritchard replied. "Do you know where she's working?"

"I haven't got a clue. I heard it was someplace in Beaver Dam, but I don't know where."

"I guess we'll have to wait until she gets home." Pritchard shook his head. "I can't believe it. Hell, Al, if it wasn't for you, she might have gotten away with it."

"Yeah, well I can't believe that Battoon didn't check it out," Monroe replied.

"I thought he had followed through after he talked to Fuller."

"Do you think that Patrick Fuller was covering for her or made a mistake about the night?" Monroe asked.

"I don't know who made the error. Perhaps, Battoon got his dates wrong. Right now, it's hard to say. But, whatever happened, Gloria and Fuller stayed at that motel on the seventeenth, not the eighteenth." He thought for a moment. "Who's on patrol tonight?"

"Barry and that new guy," Monroe told him.

"Tell Barry I want him to do a drive-by every half hour or so until he sees some lights on in Gloria's house," Pritchard instructed. "I'll pick her up as soon as she gets home."

"She's either living in the dark or she's out of town, but there's been no activity in that house for two days now," Monroe stated.

"And, she's not answering her phone. It's still going straight to voice mail," Pritchard said as he ended the latest attempt to call Gloria. "I guess she could be out of town for the holidays."

"Why don't you give Mark a call? He might know if she's out of town," Deputy Monroe suggested.

"He doesn't know where she's working so I doubt he knows where she is. I guess it wouldn't hurt to ask him, though. I'll take a walk over there."

"Bring me back a cruller, will you?" Monroe yelled

as Pritchard walked to the door.

"Mark doesn't sell bakery goods, Al."

"I just thought... Never mind."

Five minutes later, Chief Pritchard walked back into the Police Station. "Come with me," he shouted at Deputy Monroe.

Monroe grabbed his jacket and followed Pritchard to his squad car. "What's up?"

"I think Gloria has skipped town. Mark hasn't seen or talked to her in a couple of weeks and he has no idea if or where she is working. I think we better go check out her house."

"Do you think something has happened to her?" Monroe asked.

"Not really. I think she's probably out of town, but we should still check it out. I want to see if her house is dusty. The more dust, the longer she's been gone."

Deputy Monroe glanced over at him. "I never heard that before. Couldn't her house be dusty even if she was still there?"

"Gloria is fastidious. There's no way she'd live in a dusty house."

They knew the minute they walked into the house. They didn't have to see it – they could smell it. They had smelled death before. There was no mistaking the fact that somewhere in that house there was a rotting corpse.

Gloria was in the bathtub. The little amount of water that was left in the tub was a pinky red, colored by her blood. A razor blade, lying next to the tub, was obviously what she had used to slice her wrists.

"Be careful where you walk," Pritchard said quietly.

"I know," Monroe replied. "How long do you think she's been dead?"

"I'm not even going to guess, Al. Let's get out of here. I need to call Dr. Triggs."

"Do you think she killed herself?"

"Probably. There's no sign of a struggle. I'd say that's a good guess, but we'll let the coroner confirm it one way or the other."

"Most likely, it was guilt," Monroe mumbled. "She probably couldn't live with what she'd done. Guilt probably drove her to do this."

Chief Pritchard sighed. "She could be a real bitch at times, Al, but I liked her. She was feisty and she had a good sense of humor. So, unless someone walks into the Police Station and confesses, I guess we'll never know who murdered Samantha Carlson and Gary Handler."

"Yeah, like that would ever happen," Monroe said, sarcastically.

Chapter Thirty-two

"I wonder why Gloria didn't leave a note," Chief Pritchard mentioned. "It wasn't like her not to have the last word."

"Yeah, she did like to mouth off, didn't she?" Deputy Monroe agreed, smiling. "It's sad, though, isn't it?"

"What's that, Al?"

"Well, I think it's pretty damn sad when nobody sees or hears from you in almost two weeks and you aren't missed. I'd sure like to think someone would come checking on me."

"Yeah, you're right. That is pretty sad."

Deputy Monroe walked over to a small table and picked up a container of eggnog. "Want some more?" he asked Pritchard.

"Nah, it just doesn't do it for me without the booze." Pritchard sat back in his chair and put his feet up on his desk. "At least we aren't going into the new year with any unsolved murders to deal with."

"I guess. Although, I'm still having a hard time wrapping my head around the idea that Gloria killed those people." He took a sip of his eggnog. "Or, herself, for that matter," he added.

Chief Pritchard stared at him. "Don't go there, Al. Those cases are closed. Let it be."

"I know, Charlie. But, isn't there something way down deep in your gut that tells you she didn't do it?"

Pritchard didn't say anything.

"There is, isn't there? You feel it, too."

Pritchard sighed. "Feeling it and knowing it are two different things, Al."

"I know. I'll tell you one thing, though. I'll be keeping my eye on Mark Starckweather from now on."

Pritchard smiled. "You do that. Are you going to church tonight?"

"I have to. My kids are in the show."

"The show?" Pritchard asked. "Since when do churches put on Christmas Eve shows?"

"You know what I meant. What about you?"

"The family is in town. "We'll open a few gifts tonight, but we do most of our celebrating on Christmas Day."

"My shift is almost over. Do you mind if I cut out early?"

"Go ahead. Nothing is going on here. Enjoy your show," Pritchard told him, grinning.

"Merry Christmas, Charlie," Deputy Monroe said, grabbing his jacket and heading towards the door. He turned and looked back at Pritchard. "Did you hear if it's supposed to snow?"

"I don't think so. I guess we won't be having a white Christmas this year. Merry Christmas, Al."

Mark Starckweather was sitting behind his desk enjoying a shot of Jack. He wasn't in a hurry to go home. It was Christmas Eve and he was alone. He had no family left in Columbus and no one to share the holiday with. He had locked the front door, turned off the tree lights, and decided to get drunk.

He glanced over at an oversized credenza and smiled. It held several presents that he had received from a few friends and past clients. Deciding it was time to check them out, he walked over and picked up a nicely wrapped gift. "Well, Merry Fucking Christmas to me," he mumbled, as he tore the paper off of the gift and opened it. "Shit!" he yelled and dropped the box on the floor. He was staring down at a ten-inch kitchen knife covered in dried blood.

Sven Petersen was just a few miles away from Columbus. He had promised his wife that he would be back in time to enjoy Christmas breakfast with her and her family in Rockford. He glanced at the clock on the dashboard. No sweat. It was early. He had plenty of time.

He was avoiding the town tonight and coming in a back way to the house. And, to be on the safe side, he was driving his wife's car. He felt cramped driving it, even though he had moved the seat back as far as it would go. Height may have its advantages, but not when you're almost seven feet tall and driving a mid-sized vehicle.

This would be his last trip to Columbus. He was here for Samantha. This is what she wanted.

At exactly ten-twenty, forty radio pages alerted the volunteer firefighters that a fire was in progress. One minute later, the sirens went off informing the town that something was on fire.

Chief Pritchard checked his pager, apologized to his guests, and kissed his wife on the cheek. "Don't wait up," he told her as he hurried out the door.

Deputy Monroe ran out of the house, jumped in his car, and headed towards the fire station. He called Pritchard's cell and yelled, "What's on fire?" when

Pritchard answered his phone.

"It's the Carlson house," Pritchard told him.

"Where's that?"

"The Carlson...It's the Box House, Al."

"Oh. Okay. How many have responded?" Monroe asked.

"It looks like we should have enough men."

"Good. I'll see you out there."

Sven Petersen pulled over to the side of the road and got out of the car. He looked back and watched the flames dancing on the roof of the house. He could hear the sirens wailing in the distance. He smiled sadly. The house would be way beyond saving by the time the fire trucks got there. Tears filled his eyes as he thought about Sam and Gary. "What a waste," he murmured.

As he got back into the car, he decided to take Hwy. 151 to I-90. It would be faster and better lit. He turned the car around and drove past the burning house, pulling over to the side of the road as the fire engines hurried by. He waited until he was sure no more traffic was coming and continued to the center of town. He turned left on Ludington and headed south. As he passed Starckweather Realty, he noticed a light was on in the building.

He wiped his fingerprints off of the knife and let it drop to the floor. He checked to make sure nothing had been missed and walked out of the building. He breathed in the cold air and smiled as a few flakes of fresh snow fell onto his jacket. *Looks like we might have a white Christmas after all*, he thought as he got into his car and drove away.

191

Chapter Thirty-three

"It's getting hotter than hell out there," Chief Pritchard announced, as he walked into the police station.

"It sure is," Monroe agreed. "I heard it could hit eighty today. That's warm for May."

"Anything going on?" Pritchard asked.

"Not much. The mail came. There's something for you from the Chicago Police Department," he said as he handed Pritchard a letter.

"I wonder what that could be." Chief Pritchard commented as he opened the envelope. He removed the contents and started to read the first page. He walked over to his desk, sat down, and looked over at Monroe. "Well, I'll be a son of a bitch," he exclaimed.

"What is it?" Monroe asked.

"Do you remember last fall when I called and asked the CPD if they could give me some background information on Samantha Carlson?"

"Yeah. That was over six months ago. Don't tell me you're just now hearing from them?"

"Listen to this. Samantha Carlson's mother's name was Sarah Carlson who was... You won't believe this, Al. She was the granddaughter of John Box."

"You're kidding," he said, surprised. "So, that makes Samantha..."

"John Box's great-granddaughter," Pritchard interrupted. "I can't believe it. She never said a word to anyone about this." He shook his head in disbelief. "Now it starts to make sense why she bought that house. She wanted to get back to her roots. Damn!"

"Well, if that was the reason she bought that house, it sure proves me wrong," Monroe declared.

"Whattaya mean, it proves you wrong?"

"I never said anything, but I could never understand why she bought that place. As far as we knew, she didn't have any relatives or friends living around here. So, why move from Chicago to a small town where you have no connections? It didn't make sense to me at all. Somehow, in the back of my mind, I always figured that she was hoping to find a stash of money that Carlos Moretti might have buried someplace out there," Monroe told him.

"You're kidding. You actually thought there was money buried out there?" Pritchard said grinning.

"I know it's dumb. But, she did dig up a good deal of that backyard and she said she was looking for treasure."

"She was joking, Al."

"I know that now. But, at the time, I figured it was possible. Moretti never got back to that place after the Feds arrested him. He could have had some money hid away. It never crossed my mind that old John Box was her great-granddaddy."

"I figure if there was any money there, somebody would have found it a long time ago. The Feds went through that place with a fine-tooth comb after they arrested Moretti. There's no way they could have missed it." He sat back in his chair and looked up at the ceiling. "I wonder how many times the Starckweathers bought and sold that place," Pritchard contemplated.

"It was a lot. It seems like you always saw a for-sale sign out front when you drove by."

193

"Do you realize that this is the first time in over a hundred and fifty years that this town doesn't have a Starckweather living in it?"

"Yeah, but Mark would have been the last one anyway. I wonder why him and Gloria never had any kids."

"It's probably best they didn't. The way those two fought, those kids would never have been normal," Pritchard said.

"Sometimes, I wonder if Gloria really committed suicide or if it was Mark that did it."

"You know what, Al? I think that was all Gloria. I mean, why wouldn't Mark confess to killing all three of them if he had killed Gloria, too? Nah, I don't think he killed her. Never did."

"It's kinda weird, though, that both Mark and Gloria killed themselves."

"Well, at least Mark left a note." He glanced at the letter from the CPD again. "According to this letter, Samantha was the last of the Box family."

"It's strange when you drive down River Road now. You know, seeing an empty lot where that house stood. I still haven't got used to it," Monroe said.

"Do you think anyone will buy that place?" Pritchard asked Monroe.

"I guess someone looking for land might." He shook his head no, changing his mind. "Nah, I don't think it will ever sell. Hell, I bet that Petersen guy couldn't give it away.

"I'm glad that house burned down. A lot of misery took place in that house."

"And, murders," Monroe added. "My God, more people were killed in that house than the rest of this

194

town put together. You would almost think it had been cursed or something."

"I think it was. I think Ray Slitzer cursed that house," Pritchard said seriously.

"Who's Ray Slitzer?"

"He married John Box's daughter, Gretchen. The story goes that he had a pretty bad temper and used her for a punching bag. One night he just disappeared. People say he took off with some woman, but no one could say who she was. I've always thought that John Box killed him and buried him out back in that field someplace."

"Are you serious?"

"I am totally serious. Hell, Al, people are living here that won't go near that place at night. They think it's haunted."

"The house is gone. It burned down. So, what is there to be afraid of now?"

"It wasn't just the house that's haunted. It's the entire property. I've had a lot of calls from people saying they've seen weird things out there late at night."

"I've never had any phone calls like that." Monroe stared at him. "You're pulling my leg, aren't you, Charlie?"

Pritchard shrugged. "Believe what you want."

"You know that there's no such thing as ghosts," Monroe declared, dead serious.

"So, you don't believe in ghosts or spirits?"

"Hell, no," Monroe said emphatically. He finished off his coffee and put the cup down. "Aren't ghosts and spirits the same thing?"

"No, they're not. Ghosts stay in one place and spirits can move from one place to another."

Monroe looked at Pritchard and grinned. "You're full of it. Besides, how do you know so much about it?"

Pritchard shrugged. "I've had a few visits from my mother."

"No way," Monroe exclaimed.

"I have an idea. How about you meet me out there at midnight?" Pritchard asked him, holding back a smile.

"Do you mean out at the Box House?"

"Yeah. Why not? We could do a little stroll around the property and see for ourselves."

"I don't think so," Monroe told him.

"Why not? Come on, Al. I mean, who knows what ghosts could be floating around out there? Hell, we might even run into Samantha and Gary while we're there. So, whattaya say? Are we on, then? The Box House at midnight?"

Deputy Monroe shook his head no. "Not if you paid me a million dollars, Charlie. No way in hell."

"And, you call yourself my deputy."

Monroe glanced over at him, looking confused. "What the hell did you mean when you said you've had visits from your mother? Your mother's not dead."

Chapter Thirty-four

Samantha looked over at Gary. "Who could that be at this time of night?"

"How should I know? It's your house."

Samantha sighed. "Are you going to answer it?"

"Nope. You get it."

Samantha stood up and gave Gary a dirty look. 'Sometimes, you are so frickin' lazy." She walked into the kitchen and answered the back door.

"Who is it?" Gary called out. He waited a moment for a reply. "Sam, is everything okay?"

"I'm afraid not, Gary," Samantha said as she walked into the living room.

"What the hell," Gary shouted, jumping out of his chair. "What's going on? What are you doing with that gun?" He stared at Samantha. "What is she doing here?"

"I have no idea," Samantha told him, tears welling up in her eyes.

Gary stared at the woman who was standing directly behind Samantha. "What do you want?" Gary yelled.

Without saying a word, the woman hit Samantha on the side of the head with the butt of the gun.

"No," he yelled, as Samantha slumped down on the floor.

The woman raised her arm, aimed the gun, and pulled the trigger. Gary was dead before he hit the floor.

"One down," she mumbled to herself. She looked down at

Samantha and grinned. "Now, it's your turn, bitch." She walked into the kitchen and grabbed an iron skillet off of the stove. As she started back into the living room, she noticed a set of knives on the counter. She smiled as she picked the largest one and walked back to where Samantha was laying on the floor. She laid the knife down on the coffee table and bent down next to Samantha.

She felt a moment of panic when Samantha suddenly opened her eyes and stared at her.

"Why?" Samantha moaned, tears filling her eyes.

Gloria only hesitated for a moment before she grasped the skillet with both hands and slowly raised it over her head.

About the Author

I was born in Idaho in 1939. My father's job demanded that we frequently move and, by the age of ten, I had lived in Idaho, Montana, Colorado, Michigan, and Wisconsin.

I am the proud mother of three wonderful sons and two fantastic grandsons. I have no plans to acquire another husband, as they are just too much work.

Most of my life, I worked as an accountant. Two years before I retired, I did a complete switch in careers and managed two Curves fitness facilities in Illinois. I retired in 2002 and moved to Branson, MO. In 2012, I moved to Indiana to be closer to my family and have resided in Highland since then.

I enjoy a good laugh and figure it's my sense of humor that keeps me going when times are tough. Reading has always been one of my passions and I still read a couple of books a week.

In 2014, I wrote my first book, *Blueberries and Bears and My Brother's Shoes*, a book about growing up in the forties and fifties. After I self-published it and gave it to friends and family to read, they encouraged me to get serious about my writing.

I never thought that, at the age of 75, I would become an author. I set a goal for myself to write at least ten books before I die. I've made the ten plus and I'm pretty sure I have a lot more stories kicking around in this head of mine.

I certainly am enjoying my retirement knowing, when I get up each morning, I have something to look forward to. You can find out more about me and my books at www.susanlpare.com. Please visit me there, sign up to be on my readers' list, and feel free to send me your comments.

www.ingramcontent.com/pod-product-compliance
Lightning Source LLC
Chambersburg PA
CBHW071908220626
47052CB00002B/254